GW01403302

Fate's Gamble

Mafia's Children, Volume 4

Amara Holt

Published by Amara Holt, 2024.

PROLOGUE

Matteo

11 YEARS OLD

"**D**arling, this is all a big mistake," my mother's voice echoed through the house.

I pretended that my headphones were turned up loud enough to drown out their conversation, but in reality, I heard everything.

"You really think I trust you? You're just a woman. Between your word and my father's, I believe his," my father spat, as if he were the owner of the truth.

"You know I love you and would never do something like this," she said, trying to catch a glimpse of their argument from the corner of her eyes.

"Love? Those who love don't betray," my father spat again, fiercely.

"Don't you see this was your father's setup?" Without even giving me a chance to blink, my father's hand was already clamped around my mother's neck, squeezing her skin tightly, turning her face red.

"Never say that my father would set something like this up," my father roared at my mother, pushing her against the wall and banging her head there.

"DAD." Without thinking, I pulled off my headphones and jumped off the couch.

He didn't release my mother; he just turned his eyes towards me, squinting as if he were a man in the skin of a murderous wolf.

1

"Matteo, stay and watch how a man of the house solves his problems." Revealing a wicked smile, he tightened his grip on my mother's neck further, my eyes locking with hers.

"Mom isn't lying, I was with her, I saw when that man approached..."

"SHUT UP, MATTEO!!!" my father yelled, hitting my mother's face against the wall again.

My body trembled at the sight of my mother moaning in pain, her dark eyes filled with the redness of tears.

"Matt..." My mother tried to call my name but was unable to because my father was squeezing her neck tighter and tighter.

"Matteo, are you saying your grandfather lied? He was the one who made me see the scene right before my eyes." My father turned his face towards me, but what troubled me the most was that unyielding grip on my mother's neck, he never released it.

"No, Dad, what I'm saying is that I was with Mom, I saw when that man approached and grabbed her violently, he kissed her forcefully," I defended her.

"Never trust a woman," my father said in a way that frightened me, he seemed consumed by an unmatched rage.

"But Dad..."

"Enough, Matteo, your mother is a liar, just like all the women on this earth. The day I believe in a woman, you can consider me a dead man, because I'll take my own life," he growled, punching my mother's head against the wall again.

She moaned, her eyes slowly closing right in front of mine, and I witnessed my mother collapse. My father would kill her if he didn't let go.

I ran towards them. With my fists clenched, with all the strength I had in me, I pushed him away brutally, without thinking of the consequences, making my father stagger back and releasing my mother, who fell to the floor.

"You little worm," my father roared.

But I paid no attention to anything he said, I just knelt beside my mother, who slowly opened her eyes and started coughing as if trying to catch her breath.

"Carlo knows I love you, knows I do everything I can to keep you calm." My mother barely seemed to see me there beside her.

"Damn love, traitorous love." From the corner of my eye, I saw my father draw a gun from his waist.

"Dad, no," I whispered, pleading.

"I'm only not killing you because you're my heir." His eyes met mine, but my body didn't tremble; all I wanted was to protect my mother.

"Darling, I love you..." My mother's phrase died when that deafening noise echoed, the shot made everything go silent. I closed my eyes, opening them quickly right after.

Those were my mother's last words, meant for the man who killed her; I wished they had been for me, but they weren't. My mother hadn't even looked at me.

As if everything were moving in slow motion, I saw the red blood seep into the living room carpet. Kneeling beside her, I witnessed her eyes closed, the center of her forehead with that small hole.

It was my mother; I knew she loved me, she was a good woman, always doing everything for me.

"Oh, God, what have I done?" My father let his gun fall to the floor. "Donna... wake up, Donna..."

Carlo knelt beside me, his movement causing me to fall to the side as my hands touched the carpet and sank gently into her blood. I lifted my mother, feeling the blood on my fingers, watching it stain them.

"Donna, wake up... wake up." My father started shaking her body.

This wasn't the first time they fought; my grandfather was always somehow involved. It didn't take a genius to know he didn't want them together. But Carlo trusted his father blindly to doubt. Even in that moment of vulnerability, once he regained his sadistic consciousness, he would probably take pride in having killed the woman he believed was unfaithful.

Pulling back, I rubbed my hands on my pants, trying to wipe off the blood that had stained them, and stood up.

I saw my father kneeling beside my mother, shaking her body, futilely begging her to wake up.

What I feared most had happened, my greatest fear became real—during one of his fits of rage, Dad killed Mom. He couldn't control himself; he was trained to be a killer and killed my mother, the woman who loved us. She even seemed to love her husband more than she loved me. As if all his madness, all his imbalances weren't enough to hate him, but to love him instead.

Was that love? Was love making people sick? All I saw before me were two sick people: my father for killing his wife, and my mother for loving her aggressor. I knew they loved each other, but it was a sick love, a love I didn't want in my life.

Maybe I never wanted to love someone at that level, or maybe I would never allow myself to be with a woman, to never risk being in a situation like this.

CHAPTER ONE

Billie

Years Later...

Pretending to be a happy family had become easy over the years. Easy didn't mean enjoyable. I hated being around my family for these kinds of events.

Cassandra Harris didn't care about anything but her appearance and reputation among all the famous circles she was in. James Harris might be different; if his only concern wasn't his own nose, nothing else mattered, as if only my father's pains were important.

Spending almost my entire childhood and adolescence at boarding school wasn't the best way to get a sense of a loving family. I had some friends, but most of them were opportunistic; being a Harris made everyone think how privileged I was.

Sometimes I just wanted to know what it was like to have present parents, to have a Christmas like those romantic comedies where everyone woke up on Sunday morning to open presents.

"Did you have to wear those heels?" Mom whispered, leaning her ear close to mine.

"What's wrong with them?" I questioned, lowering my face to look at my red stilettos.

"You know how much I hate being extraordinarily taller than you, and here you come with these tiny heels," she complained, twisting her lip.

"I was asked to be here for this event. I'm here now, and as for my outfit, let me handle it," I retorted, grabbing another glass of champagne from the tray the waiter was passing by. "And if you don't like it, I'll leave right now."

"Ungrateful girl," Mom murmured.

"I learned from the best." I flashed the most forced smile I could manage.

Just then, a photographer approached, holding a glass of champagne in one hand, placing the other hand on my mother's waist, and smiled for the photograph that was taken.

Once the man left, I looked back at Mom.

"Why is this event so important?" I asked, watching Mom look around.

"The opening of this grand hotel has two major directors as guests, who are about to do a highly acclaimed adaptation of a best-selling book," her eyes even sparkled as she talked about it.

"And how did Cassandra Harris know about this? She immediately made sure to get a reservation to be here," my tone was completely mocking.

"It was easy; the president was a cutie." She bit the corner of her mouth, making me roll my eyes.

"I wonder how you managed to include Dad in these reservations."

"Sweetie, powerful men don't want wives, just a good fuck, and that's something I know how to do very well." Cassandra shrugged her shoulders.

"Wow, what pride," I whispered dramatically.

Actually, I wasn't surprised; I grew up knowing my parents weren't normal. When I was home, I saw people coming and going all the time. They had what seemed like an open relationship, but in front of their fans, they were faithful. A united family, totally structured, the kind of marriage everyone aspired to. Little did they know what I witnessed.

What surprised me most in my entire life, or even made me certain of something I had always suspected, was when, at eighteen, I came home unannounced and saw Dad with another man on our living room sofa. I realized something I had always felt: Dad was bisexual, as I had seen him with women besides Mom.

That day, they both called me for a talk. They said they had an open marriage but didn't want their fans to know. That revelation wasn't a big secret; I spent my childhood hearing them talk about a friend coming over, a friend I had never seen.

I might have been a child, but I wasn't naive; I knew they weren't just friends but lovers, fleeting affairs. I didn't know what a real marriage was like; all I saw was a completely wrong relationship.

But according to them, they loved each other. If that was love, I don't think I had the maturity to experience love.

"How are my girls?" Dad approached at that moment.

"Did you get anything?" Mom ignored his question, asking another instead.

"Not much to get. Jared is a very reserved man; I couldn't even get close to him." Dad ran his hand through his hair, pushing it back.

"That's because you don't know how to do the job right. How about the three of us go?" Cassandra's eyes sparkled again.

"Let's go." The two of them took each other's hands and gave a nod for us to follow.

We approached a small group of four men in suits; one of them must have been the director they were so eager to meet.

I stopped next to my father, watching another waiter pass by with a tray of champagne. I left my empty glass there and took a full one; if I had to endure this, it might as well be with some good champagne.

I took a sip of the liquid and felt the tiny, delicate bubbles explode deliciously in my mouth.

Dad greeted the men, all of whom he knew, introducing me to everyone with pride in his voice, as if he were presenting "the" perfect family.

"Did you follow in your parents' artistic footsteps, Billie?" one of the men asked me, as if I were close to him, even though my father hadn't bothered to introduce anyone.

"As my mother says, I'd be much happier if I had. But no, I recently graduated in fashion design." I forced a smile, or rather, a strained grin.

"In a way, you're still on the same path. Do you plan to work for celebrities?" The man, whose name I still didn't know, asked curiously.

"I haven't decided yet, but I don't think so. Growing up in this world has made me certain I don't belong to it." I shrugged, knowing how much my words would irritate Cassandra.

For those who asked her, Mom bragged about how her only daughter loved all the glamour that fame provided, when it was actually the opposite.

Maybe the alcohol was going to my head, and possibly the filter was going with it.

"Billie is too modest to admit how much she loves all this." Mom waved her hand, gesturing to the luxurious event we were at.

"Oh, Mom, please, you know I'm shy," I lied, glancing at her over my father's shoulder.

"Whether she admits it or not, it's a shame that someone born to two splendid actors doesn't follow the same path," the man continued, eliciting one of Mom's soft, restrained laughs she always gave when she wanted to show off.

"Thank you, dear." Mom patted Dad's jacket as if she wished it were that man.

The two of them repulsed me. As a child, I had no choice but to partake in their horror show. But at 22, I didn't know why I still bothered to be there. Maybe there was a part of me that, futilely, wanted to be with my parents, for them to act like parents.

But as always, I was bitterly disappointed. Cassandra and James always put their careers first, and last, when it was necessary to parade their perfect daughter, they thought of me.

"If you'll excuse me, I'm going to the bar," I said with a restrained smile, making my exit before Mom could block me.

Luckily, she was too engrossed in her new conversation, and I managed to escape.

CHAPTER TWO

Billie

"Please, give me your strongest drink," I said, sitting on one of the high stools and placing my purse on the bar counter.

"Are you sure, miss?" The bartender gave a small smile as if mocking my request.

"Do I look like I'm bluffing?" I raised an eyebrow.

"Would you like me to call someone?" What a tedious man.

"Just give me the damn drink, or is it hard to understand?" I asked, trying not to get even more irritated.

"Sorry for the inconvenience, it's just that girls like you don't usually drink like this." He turned away when he saw me roll my eyes.

"Girls like me," I muttered, as if girls like me were reserved and should at least come from a structured family, not a messed-up one like mine.

Finally, the bartender brought me the drink. It was transparent, almost like water, but the way the ice moved inside and the small straw revealed it wasn't just water.

I took the glass in my hand, didn't even think about it, just held my breath and drank it all in one gulp. I grimaced as the burn traveled down my throat, my eyes closed, tears welled up, and everything seemed to burn.

"Miss, are you okay?" The bartender's voice brought me back to reality.

I blinked a few times, clearing the tears. I gave a brief smile.

"Couldn't be better. I need another one of these." I pushed the empty glass, wanting more.

"But miss, this is pure cachaça..."

"Great, then I want more cachaça. That's the only way to tolerate all that show-off; after all, that's all I am," I complained, knowing the man probably didn't understand a word I said.

At least he turned away with the glass. I ran my hand through my hair, tossing it back.

"Can I sit here?" a deep voice entered my ear. I turned my face and saw a tall man, maybe I had stared too long at his imposing stature, as he asked again, "Or not?"

"Sit down, after all, this stool isn't mine." I gestured with my hand.

"It's a stool," he corrected.

"Whatever, as long as you keep your butt on it." I shrugged, watching the bartender place another glass of the transparent liquid on the counter.

"Get me another one, please." The man next to me pushed his empty glass.

"Whiskey?"

"Yes." I found myself studying the features of the man beside me. His hair was tied in a bun, with the color underneath near his nape appearing to be dark brown, with a few golden streaks, suggesting he was someone who spent a lot of time in the sun, lightening a few strands, while his golden skin revealed a natural tan.

"I have the impression I know you from somewhere," he said.

"I don't trust my instincts at the moment, but men with long hair aren't part of the prerequisites for being in my bed, so no, we probably don't know each other." I took the glass, knowing that wasn't really me talking, and I probably wouldn't be proud of it the next day.

"You only talk to men you'll sleep with?" he asked again.

"And do you have any other purpose besides that?" I asked back.

"It's hard to defend my kind, especially coming from someone like me." The bartender brought his drink.

I watched him take it to his mouth. He had a beard that perfectly framed his face, apparently well-groomed, not too long, but not too short; I'd describe it as medium.

But there was something inside me trying to remind me. But I was almost sure I didn't know him.

"Did you find what you were looking for?" the man beside me asked, catching me off guard.

"Actually, no." I turned forward, taking the glass and drinking it all like the first time.

One gulp, my eyes closing, my mouth twisting. At least this time, my eyes didn't fill with tears.

"What makes a person drink like this?" the guy next to me asked.

"You're drinking too, so—" I left the sentence unfinished for him to interpret as he wished.

"I have my reasons."

"So do I." I pushed my glass towards the bartender as he walked by. "Another one..."

"I have to—"

"If you finish that sentence, I swear I'll make you swallow that glass," I snapped, not even letting him finish his thought.

The guy next to me flashed a brief smile. It wasn't just any smile; it was a sexy one that made my legs go weak. Luckily, I was sitting down.

"On top of everything, you're angry. What's wrong? Did you end a relationship? Were you betrayed?" The guy next to me wanted to know.

"I wish it were that simple, but to be betrayed, I'd need to be in a relationship. Men are more like objects to me, just as we women are to them," I said, while he finished his drink and ordered another.

"So, what's your reason?" he asked.

"My parents, two assholes," I grumbled, shrugging my shoulders.

"Haven't heard the word 'assholes' in a long time." He didn't take his eyes off me.

"And what's your reason? Are you going to tell me you're an alcoholic?" I spoke with a hint of mockery.

"Maybe I'm becoming one." His eyes seemed to wander off, as if reflecting on his memories. "I got an invitation to my ex-fiancée's wedding; she's getting married, but not to me."

The guy looked back at me, and at that moment, his eyes glinted with a mischievous sparkle in my direction.

"Should I congratulate you for escaping a wedding, or are you crying because you were replaced?" I asked, confused.

"You can congratulate me. I was the one who ended it. I told her to find someone else. The perfect family Juliana wanted couldn't be me to provide."

"But deep down, you're resentful. You didn't want to see her with someone else, and it seems like she moved on and found someone who could give her everything," I reflected, joining in his conversation.

Together, we raised our glasses, clinking them on the table, and ordered another round of drinks. At least this way, I was away from the two of them.

CHAPTER THREE

Billie

I looked back, my eyes fixing on my mother as she approached.

"Damn it," I muttered.

"What's the problem?" the guy with the long hair wanted to know.

We had been talking for a few minutes and hadn't even introduced ourselves. It wasn't necessary, after all; two slightly drunk people wouldn't remember what happened the next day.

"My mom. I'm sure she's coming over to give one of her sermons. I don't know why I still hope that at some point, they could just be normal parents," I grumbled to the guy next to me.

"I'm not the best person to give an opinion about that." He tried to look back, searching for what I had mentioned.

"Don't look," I retorted, poking his arm and feeling its firm strength.

"Do you want to get out of here?" he asked quickly.

"Can we go to a hotel? Far from here." I pouted.

"Go to a hotel with a man you just met?" The long-haired guy looked horrified at my request.

"Are you going to kill me?" I asked, standing up too quickly from the stool, needing to hold onto his arms as I realized I might be too tipsy.

"I don't usually kill anyone without a reason." He stood up, putting his hand on my waist to keep me upright.

"I don't usually give anyone a reason to kill me," I mimicked his way of speaking. "Come on, long hair, I need to get out of here. I don't want to run into my mom."

Without questioning, he started walking. Maybe his stature was a bit taller than I expected when he sat next to me. It was clear he was a tall man, but as he walked beside me, my face was almost touching his shoulder, making it evident.

We passed by the event entrance and soon arrived at the reception of the luxurious hotel.

"Are you staying here?" I asked.

"Yes, I am."

"Then let's go somewhere else. I don't want to risk being spotted." I pulled the man's hand, which he kindly held around my waist again, trying to keep me steady.

"Where are we going?" he asked as we passed through the revolving doors.

"This is Las Vegas, baby. We can do anything, with one exception: we should stay away from wedding chapels. We're too drunk to end up married," I joked, walking down the sidewalk and feeling the night breeze against my body.

"Definitely, we should stay away from weddings." His firm hands made me want to trip on purpose just to be caught by them.

"Where are you from, long hair? You're clearly not from around here. Your English has some flaws," I teased with a smile.

"You guessed it, I'm from Italy, specifically Sicily."

"Cool. I have a friend who married an Italian." Thinking about Yulia made everything more bittersweet, as I missed her terribly.

"Why does everything revolve around this word, 'marriage'? The world would be much better without weddings." The way he wrinkled his nose was somewhat amusing.

"I love weddings. I wanted to get married, but I don't believe in love, not with the experiences I've had or witnessed. I'd definitely prefer to die alone with three hundred cats to take care of," I declared, stepping away from the long-haired guy and spinning around on the brightly lit street filled with neon lights decorating the establishments.

Everything here was so magical; magic was something I wanted for my life.

"Girl." I felt the long-haired guy's grip on my wrist, pulling me back. "Are you crazy? You're spinning around and showing your underwear to everyone."

"Oh, that would be a huge displeasure for Mom." I turned my face to meet the brown eyes of the tall man. "Do you know what would make me just like her?"

"What?" he asked, not taking his eyes off me.

"Going to bed with a complete stranger." I gave a mischievous smile.

"I'm not sure if that would be a good idea; we're drunk..."

"No, we're too sober. How about we go to that bar, drink until we forget our names, you to forget your Juliana and me to forget my crazy parents." I raised my hand, touching his beard, which was surprisingly soft.

He seemed to consider the idea, looking over my shoulder at the bar glowing with colorful lights.

"We're in Las Vegas, long hair. We're two strangers just trying to hide from our problems." I continued, urging him to go along with this madness.

"No introductions?" he asked.

"None, so as not to make things awkward the next day, that is, if we end up in the same bed, which would be a big waste if we didn't." I bit the corner of my lip, letting my eyes roam over his body.

"Let's go," he replied, holding my hand as a laugh escaped my lips.

That was all I wanted—a night without memories, getting drunk enough to forget my name, and to forget another of the major disappointments I had with my parents.

If Yulia were here, she would surely calm me down, offer me her shoulder to cry on, and undoubtedly wouldn't let me take a single drop of alcohol.

But she wasn't here, and as always, I didn't know how to deal with my problems. That's why I preferred to drown my sorrows with a stranger I had just met.

The long-haired guy stepped in front of me and held the door open for me to enter. I looked around; it was a dimly lit bar with a few pool tables and couples sitting at corner tables that looked like they were made of leather.

We walked to one of the counters. I pulled out a stool and sat on it, watching him sit next to me with one of his feet propped up on the footrest. It was amazing how this man became more attractive, wearing a black button-up shirt with the top buttons undone, and black dress pants that fit his toned legs perfectly. *What a big man, was all I could keep repeating to myself.*

"What would you like to drink?" the bartender asked, stopping in front of the counter.

"We want whatever you have that's the strongest," I said first, looking at the long-haired guy, waiting for him to say something.

"Sure," he agreed when he realized we were waiting for his approval.

"Can we make just one promise?" I asked, knowing I was about to do something reckless.

"Say it, Barbie," the way he called me made me roll my eyes.

"Regardless of anything, let's promise each other not to end the night married and not to let the other end up with any other stranger," I requested, watching him look thoughtful.

"So, one takes care of the other?"

"Yes, exactly."

"No marriages?" The way he pursed his lips made me smile widely.

"None, please..." I shook my head vehemently.

The clinking of glasses made us look forward to see our drinks.

"Let the games begin," I declared, holding my glass first.

CHAPTER FOUR

Billie

"Ow..." I murmured, bringing my hand to my head, struggling to open my eyes.

I blinked several times, adjusting to the morning light. *It was morning, wasn't it? Wait, where was I?*

Damn, damn, damn...

Flashes of memory came to me—disheveled hair, that roar that sounded more like a wolf's, the moans and sighs... I quickly turned my face to see the man asleep next to me.

Shit, shit, shit...

How did I do this? How did I end up in the bed of a complete stranger? *No, wait! I knew him.*

At that moment, I wanted to scream at myself *...idiot, idiot, idiot!*

He was one of the men from my friend's husband, I remembered him clearly from Yulia's wedding—the way he was serious, composed, always by Valentino's side. An incredibly handsome man, and by chance, I ended up in bed with him. *And I couldn't remember anything...*

At that moment, I wanted to cry.

Did we really have sex? I would never forgive myself if I had slept with that man and couldn't remember what happened.

I lifted the covers, looked underneath, and found completely naked. I surely shouldn't have taken off my clothes just to sleep. I looked over at the man. He was wearing black boxer briefs, his chest bare, revealing his tanned, hairless skin. Dear God, how could I have slept with that Italian and not remember anything?

This was my punishment for thinking I was invincible and drinking every last drop of liquor in that bar.

I only remembered going into the bar with the long-haired guy, who I now knew was the Italian from Yulia's wedding. After we started drinking one glass after another, everything went up in smoke, and my memory went with it.

How was I going to face him when I visited my friend? Did it have to be that Italian, my chosen one? I hadn't even been away from Yulia for a month, and already I was messing up.

Gathering all my dignity or what was left of it, I slowly placed one foot on the floor at a time. I tried my best not to make noise, searched for my clothes, found my dress, put it on, grabbed my purse, and put my panties, which were on the floor, into it.

If I sneaked out without waking him, there was a good chance the Italian wouldn't even remember I was there. If his memory was like mine, I might escape unscathed, leaving only me with the recollection of that moment—or part of it if we ever met again at my friend's house.

I held my stiletto in my hand and decided to put it on only when I was outside the door.

I glanced back at the Italian. I didn't remember his name, but I knew it was him, the man who worked for that mafia connected to my friend's husband.

What a waste, how could I have been with him and not even remember anything? It was like everything was cloudy. I knew we were together, that we had drunk too much, and from the delightful numbness between my legs, I knew his cock must have been big enough to feel it the next day.

Damn! All I wanted was to remember the sex I had with that long-haired guy.

Liquor, when it doesn't kill you, humiliates you. I believed that in this case, I went through both.

I sighed silently, turned my back, and left the room without knowing where I was. There was a part of me screaming to stop doing these crazy things; I couldn't keep subjecting myself to that kind of stuff.

I wasn't proud of myself, maybe even felt a bit dirty. *Damn it, now the moral hangover was coming.*

I stopped at the wall, leaning against it while putting on my stiletto. In my purse was my phone, which I grabbed and checked the time. *Great*, it was almost noon. Fortunately, we were in Las Vegas. A city that thrived more at night.

I stopped in front of the elevator and called it. I looked through my contact list and dialed Yulia. I needed to talk to her, needed my other person, the one who understood me better than anyone else.

The phone rang several times before she answered:

"Billie, is something wrong?" Yulia's voice indicated she had just woken up.

"Sorry, did I wake you?" I asked as I entered the elevator.

"It's early here, friend," Yulia said, sounding like she was moving, as if she were walking. "But go ahead, we promised each other we'd call in any emergency, even if it was in the middle of the night. Now tell me, what happened?"

"I messed up, big time, and now I'm interrupting your honeymoon..."

"Just don't tell me you married a complete stranger?"

"No, well, I don't think so." I bit my lip. "Yulia, I slept with a man, a man I shouldn't have slept with."

"Which man are we talking about exactly?"

The elevator doors opened, and I walked out into the hotel lobby, knowing I wasn't staying there. I headed towards the exit and got into the first taxi I saw. I gave the driver the address while continuing to talk to my friend.

"That long-haired guy, your husband's friend." My eyes fixed on the street as the car drove.

"The consigliere of Valentino?" Yulia sounded surprised.

"What's an Italian doing in Las Vegas? What a small world," I muttered, grumbling.

"Look, I don't know, but I can ask Valentino. All I know is they have an extension of their headquarters there, they have business—if I'm not mistaken, it's a nightclub."

"Great, indeed a small world," I grumbled again. "Could you check with your husband about this consigliere? It would be much better if he didn't remember anything, so we could avoid all the embarrassments I must have gone through last night."

"What do you mean? Didn't he see you leaving?"

"No, he was sleeping like the sexy beast he is, and I don't remember a thing," I whined, lightly banging my head against the car window.

"Billie Harris! You really don't consider the consequences, friend, how can you get to this point?"

"I messed up, I really messed up," I murmured, closing my eyes against the throbbing pain in my head.

"I'll find out what I can from Valentino and then tell you everything. But Billie, please, don't do this kind of thing again. I'm so scared, scared of not being there for you..."

"Sorry for causing all this trouble in your life. I promise I'll try to do better," I declared.

We talked a bit more about her honeymoon. Soon the car stopped in front of the hotel where she was staying. Knowing I still had to face my mother for leaving without notice, I wasn't sure if I had the patience to deal with that.

CHAPTER FIVE

Matteo

"Hell of pain," I grumbled, rubbing my eyes.

I turned over in the unfamiliar bed, seeing it disheveled beside me. What the hell did I do last night?

"Hello?" I called out a bit louder, trying to see if I was alone.

No one answered, which was a good sign. I didn't have to explain anything. I sat up, folded my legs, and looked around the empty room again.

In the middle of the pillow, a small earring caught my attention. I picked it up and held it between my fingers.

Images of the girl from last night flashed through my mind. Now sober and with a clear head, I wondered what I was thinking sitting next to that beautiful blonde. She was alone in that bar; I just wanted to keep her company.

Who was I kidding? I just wanted to fuck her.

She was beautiful, in that loose dress, with a delicate neckline and slightly full lips. I was already drunk, so whatever I did was just a drunken side of me taking over. I didn't expect us to end up in that other bar where everything literally went south.

It was drink after drink, and before I knew it, we were making out right there. I might have been drunk, but my mind managed to remember almost everything.

The way she danced in that bar, or when she tried to kiss the bartender—oh God, that blonde was literally crazy. She even asked the

23

bartender if she wanted to join us for a threesome since she'd never tried one. Obviously, that didn't happen, which was a huge relief.

Nothing would stop us; from the moment we first looked at each other, it was clear we'd end up in the same bed.

I always remembered everything, or almost everything, but not this time. I didn't know how the sex was. I wanted to remember what it was like to be in her arms. Did we even have sex? I believed we did; my cock was definitely showing signs of a good fuck.

Everything in those blue eyes screamed danger. Nothing about her was like the women I usually slept with.

I ran my hand through my hair, pulling it down and tying it up in a bun. I needed to get myself together, do what I came to Las Vegas for, and return to Sicily as soon as possible.

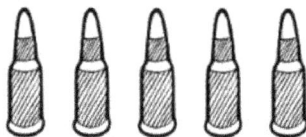

THE TAXI PULLED UP in front of the hotel where I was staying. I had only stayed there because it was closer to our nightclub. I didn't expect it to be newly opened with events and annoying people.

If there was one thing I had no patience for, it was people.

I walked through the revolving doors, and my phone vibrated in my pocket. I checked it and saw my friend's name on the screen. Besides being the Don of the Cosa Nostra, Valentino was like a friend to me.

"What's up?" I said, putting the phone to my ear.

"Just tell me it's a lie," Valentino's statement made me frown.

"We're talking about what exactly?" I asked.

"Did you go to bed with my wife's friend?" He wanted to know.

"Fuck!" I muttered, scratching my beard with my free hand. "Don't tell me that crazy blonde is her friend?"

"Matteo, you used to be the sensible one among us." Valentino let out a heavy sigh.

"That damn Juliana's wedding invitation blew all my plans to hell. How could she? It's been less than six months since we ended our engagement, and she's already getting married to someone else?" I stopped in front of the elevator.

"Simple, she moved on. You dragged her along with that engagement for years, and now she found someone who could give her what you refused to." I could swear Valentino was shrugging his shoulders at that moment.

"I wasn't ready to hear that Juliana is marrying someone else..."

"What I don't understand is why you're not going after her?" As he spoke, the elevator doors opened, and I stepped inside.

"No, I'm not getting married. I swore to myself I would never marry. If my love for her was that strong, I'd fight all my demons for Juliana. And if I have no desire to do that, it's because I don't love that woman enough," I said, repeating what I always told myself.

"So why are you still wallowing in self-pity? Why did you get so drunk that you don't even remember who you slept with?"

"Simple, all I wanted was sex, and that's what the blonde wanted too. We just had sex," I said, with more people in the elevator. Speaking Italian with Valentino, they didn't understand a thing.

"I really don't get you. I just hope this involvement of yours doesn't affect my wedding, especially now that I've managed to get a small truce with my Colombian wife." Valentino was in a marriage of convenience, all for an heir he needed, but he had a difficult Latina wife to deal with.

"There's no reason to interfere since I don't plan on seeing that crazy woman again. You should keep an eye on your wife's friends. The woman I was with last night is far from stable," I said, stepping out of the elevator and walking down the hallway to my room.

"Unstable, yet she didn't hesitate to go to bed with you..."

"Damn it!" I opened the door to my room. "I don't remember much, but I know it was her. I know the mess she caused, and I also know it must have been good sex, damn alcohol."

I headed toward the bed, sitting down and crossing one leg over the other as I took off my shoe.

"Well, just stay away from her. She's Yulia's friend, and if there's one thing I don't want to get involved with, it's the friends of my wife. We have enough conflicts without adding a new one that's not even my concern. Now, changing the subject, how are things on your end?"

"I've uncovered some leads on who's behind the threats to our clan. Today I'm going after those leads with some of our men," I declared with conviction.

The Cosa Nostra was being threatened; a small-time gang thought they could invade our territory in Las Vegas and drive us out. This happened after Valentino's honeymoon, which is why he couldn't be there. Santino, his underboss, was with his pregnant wife, so it fell to me. It wasn't the consigliere's job to be on that territory, checking those backgrounds. But for my Don, I was loyal.

I intended to find out who was behind it as soon as possible and return to Sicily, where my home and peace were. To accomplish that, I might need to stay away from women and stop thinking about wedding invitations, especially avoiding a certain blonde who loved to cause trouble.

CHAPTER SIX

Billie

The noise from the door made me squint my eyes; I just wanted to sleep. Why was it so hard for them to understand that?

"Where have you been, may I ask?" Cassandra's shrill voice came in like an annoying static in my ears.

"Out and about," I mumbled, pulling the pillow over my head and covering my ears.

"Billie Harris, don't act like a teenager," Mom's tone made me sit up in bed, looking directly at her.

"You know, Mom, I'm tired—tired of all this. I'm tired of being treated like an accessory for events. I don't want this anymore. I don't want to go out and play the perfect family when we both know we're not. I've always rushed to where you were, feeling guilty for most of my life, thinking it was my duty to be there. Meanwhile, you and Dad never cared about me, never treated me like a normal child, always just an ornament. Maybe all the exhaustion was coming out at that moment, making me explode. I'm done. I owe you nothing. I don't need to be in places where I don't feel comfortable."

Cassandra stared at me with her wide blue eyes. We looked very alike, except for the fact that she was tall and I was short. I didn't know who I inherited that height from.

"What are you talking about? We've always given you everything. You've never lacked anything." Mom began to fill her eyes with tears, putting on her best acting performance.

"I wish all those material things you gave me could be replaced with love, affection, a family Christmas..." I murmured, getting out of bed and adjusting my nightgown.

"You know we've always been very busy, especially during holidays," she always had a ready answer for everything.

"Twenty-two years old, that's my age. In my 22 years, you've never had time for me. But it's okay, Mom. I'll always love both of you for providing me with everything material. After all, I'm privileged to have a life full of material wealth. I just feel empty, emotionally empty," my voice trailed off as I headed towards the bathroom.

For the first time, Cassandra said nothing, which was a huge relief. I didn't want to discuss it any further. I entered the suite, locked the door, and leaned against it, closing my eyes and breathing heavily.

It was as if I wanted to cry, but the tears seemed to be stuck in some dark place inside me as my chest tightened, and I sat on the floor, hugging my knees.

I rested my head on my knees, bit my lip hard, and tried to inflict physical pain on myself, hoping that feeling would leave me. I wanted to cry, scream, beg for a drop of attention.

But no one would come. I had always been alone; the only person I had was my friend, and she was married now. Not that I was sad; Yulia deserved to be happy, even if it was far from me.

I needed to learn to deal with my own torment, to grow up, to stop acting like a spoiled child. I was 22, I was educated; that should be enough to take control of my life.

I stopped biting my lips, the metallic taste of blood in my mouth, my eyes as dry as a desert without rain. The tears didn't come, and the torment would continue.

Even though I tried to apply everything my therapist said, nothing seemed to work in those crises, as if everything turned cloudy, the pain of loneliness tightening my chest.

I stretched my legs on the floor of the suite, my head tilted back as I started to breathe more calmly. The minutes of anguish passed, and the moisture began to take over my eyes.

I knew the breakdown would come; first, it was the lack of reaction from my body, and then, when everything seemed to ease, the tears would come.

With my eyes still closed, I felt my face start to become damp, letting all the pain flow away with those tears.

I stayed there alone for a long time, knowing that my mom was no longer in the room. Waiting for me would be too tedious for Cassandra.

I got up from the floor, went to the sink to wash my face, not even knowing what time it was. After I got home, I just took a shower and went to bed.

Last night served as a lesson never to drink that much again. Even though I had taken painkillers for my headache, it still felt like a hangover.

I left the room to find it empty, a beautiful bouquet of flowers on the bed, with many red roses, my favorites. They would have been lovely if I didn't know who they were from.

I approached, seeing a small note next to the bouquet. With a long sigh, I picked it up and read the message:

"We're sorry for everything we've caused in your life. Know that you will always be important to us, Mom and Dad. PS: We have a family dinner tomorrow night, you're invited. It will be here at the hotel."

That was typical of them, but the part about the dinner made me believe they really wanted a family moment. My naive heart beat a little faster.

As if we were searching for any scrap.

I took the beautiful bouquet in my hand, smelled the flowers, and smiled at their scent.

I sat on the bed, took out my phone, looking for any sign of the Italian. Was it possible I'd be lucky enough for him not to remember anything? There was a part of me that wished I could be in his arms again just to know how it had been, what it must have been like to have those strong hands holding me.

I could swear he came with a roar; that Italian had a body too big for a quiet climax.

I shook my head, trying to dispel those thoughts, and prayed to God that I would forget that man as soon as possible, for I felt I was on the verge of going mad every time I thought about the night I couldn't remember anything.

I focused on that bouquet of flowers, a remnant of joy for my parents wanting that family dinner.

CHAPTER SEVEN

Billie

With one last look in the mirror, I approved of my look, loving the dress I had chosen. It was a new collection from a designer I adored.

My mother didn't even show her face in my room, only sending a message to confirm whether I would be able to attend.

I took advantage of the day alone to visit a spa in the hotel, trying my best to stay relaxed, if that was even possible. I was excited about the family dinner. It was all I had ever wanted. Would they finally understand my point of view?

I grabbed my small handbag from the bed, left the room, and my heels echoed on the floor. This time, I wore a high pair. I loved walking in heels; feeling tall occasionally was nice.

I took the elevator down to the hotel restaurant. Everything there was incredibly beautiful; whoever had built that place deserved a round of applause.

I slowly entered the restaurant, searching for my parents with my eyes. That's when I saw them, sitting at a table with other people—no, I couldn't believe it!

It was all a lie; it wasn't real at all. They said the dinner was a family event just to get me there, so they could play the happy family act.

There was no way I was going to sit at that table. My anger made my blood boil. Once again, I had fallen for their deception. Clutching my handbag tightly, I abruptly turned to leave, bumping into a hard chest...

"Damn it!" I muttered, feeling strong hands hold me at the waist to prevent me from falling to the ground from the impact.

"Are you okay? Did I hurt you?" That voice was familiar. I lifted my face, looking up at the man.

My eyes widened in shock, and clearly, his did too. Neither of us expected to see the other there.

"Italian," I murmured, somewhat dazed.

"It seems you know who I am." He raised an eyebrow slightly, not showing any smile.

"Of course, the friend of my friend's husband," the response came quickly off my tongue.

"Is that all?"

I bit the corner of my lip, lowered my head, and could even feel my face burning from embarrassment.

"Uh..." was all that came out of my mouth.

"You know, Miss," he spoke again, I felt his thumb touch my chin as he lifted my face to look in his direction. "I'm concerned about how we were together the last time. I'm concerned in many ways..."

"Well..." It seemed I had lost all ability to speak, biting my lip again.

"Don't know what to say? Is it only with alcohol in your system that you can talk?"

"Actually, the situation isn't favorable for me. I'm avoiding a situation, and having you standing here in front of me is making everything difficult." I looked around, noticing that my parents had seen me standing there, their eyes fixed on me.

"Let me guess, you're avoiding your mother?"

"You guessed it. She lied again, and I believed her." I rolled my eyes, as the good fool that I was.

"And what do you plan to do now?" His tone made it seem like he was genuinely interested.

"I don't know, run back to my room?" I shrugged my shoulders nonchalantly.

"Well, I was thinking of inviting you to have dinner with me. I need to give you some lessons." His dark brown eyes assessed me slowly, as if he were undressing me with his gaze, being explicit about each flicker of his irises, which didn't remember our night together.

"Lessons?" I frowned, confused.

"Yes." He didn't go into details, making a hand gesture for me to follow him to one of the tables. "Will you come, Billie?"

He called me by name. He knew my name, and I didn't know his.

I looked back at my parents' table. At that moment, they weren't looking at me; they were engaged in conversation with whoever, none of whom I knew.

Growing up in that world of glamour never appealed to me. I always set it as a life goal to escape it. I didn't want my child growing up far from me.

The word "child" felt too strong, as I wasn't even sure if I would be a good mother.

With a long sigh, I took the Italian's hand. My parents had lied to me, made me believe it was a family dinner when it was just another attempt to show how perfect they were. Showing them that I was there with someone else was a great way to declare that I wasn't playing around.

We approached a table. The Italian pulled out my chair, and I sat down, leaving my handbag beside me.

"Can I ask a question?" I asked, seeing him nod as he sat down next to me. He could have sat across from me, but he chose to sit beside me as if he wanted to be close. "You know my name, and I don't know yours. I'm at a disadvantage."

"That's because I received a call from Valentino, who, for some reason, already knew we had been to bed together." Our eyes met.

"I called Yulia, and since she also didn't remember your name..." I shrugged my shoulders.

"You usually call your friend like that?"

"When I looked at you and realized the mess I made, yes. Don't take it the wrong way, but we have mutual friends, and I don't want to bring any awkward situations near them..."

"Awkward is the word that defines everything you made me go through." He had his hair tied up in a low bun like last time, his well-groomed beard showcasing his lips perfectly.

"Oh, no..." I lowered my eyes, feeling embarrassed.

"You know, Billie, there are things in life where everything has limits. I'm no saint, my actions weren't right, but you were too drunk, and clearly, you don't remember anything. Should I be worried?"

"No, especially since we have nothing, and I know what I'm doing with my life." I shrugged my shoulders again, responding quickly.

"Still, no one should be in that state," he retorted.

"Are we here for a lecture?" I made a move to get up from my chair, but the Italian stopped me by holding my hand, making me sit back down.

"Theoretically, I'm just concerned, but we can change the subject. Sit down, let's talk..."

"Just talking?" I raised an eyebrow, a mischievous smile spreading across my face.

"If it doesn't involve anything alcoholic, I'd like to know how that night went..." The man gave me that intense look again, not smiling, just studying me with his eyes.

"We have a dinner ahead; we'll see how things go..."

CHAPTER EIGHT

Matteo

We placed our orders with the waiter, and Billie kept glancing nervously across the restaurant. She hadn't ordered anything alcoholic.

I slid my hand under the table and touched her leg, making her shiver.

"Look at me, forget about them," I murmured, leaning my lips close to her ear, seeing her turn her face so we could look at each other.

"You still haven't told me your name," she whispered, moistening her lips.

"Matteo De Luca." I tried to bring my lips closer to hers, wanting to taste them again, remembering the kisses Billie knew how to give, though the sex itself was still a mystery to me.

"What do you plan to do, Italian?" Our lips were almost brushing against each other when a shadow beside us made Billie pull away.

I let out an irritated sigh; I hated being interrupted, especially when I had a delicious woman beside me.

I looked up and saw a woman standing there. She was tall, a more mature version of Billie, making it clear that she was her mother.

"I think you've got the wrong table, dear!" She spoke rudely.

"Oh no, Mom, I'm exactly where I should be." Billie shrugged, and the woman turned her gaze toward me, not shy about letting her eyes roam over my chest.

"Talking about me when you're the same." Billie's mother glared at her daughter.

"It must be a family trait," Billie said, seeming unfazed. "They lied to me about it being a family dinner; I don't know why I still believe their words..."

Billie pushed back her chair and stood up, and of course, I did the same.

"Don't start with your little dramas, Billie..."

"Then get out of my way if you don't want to witness one."

Great, I was stuck in a mother-daughter argument, which I hated the most. I tried to remind myself that I was doing this for Valentino; after all, she was his wife's best friend.

I could have ignored Billie, but I spent those two damn days thinking about her, wondering what it would be like to be in her bed. I might hate her exaggerated ways, but inside me, an insatiable desire was growing.

"Let's go." I grabbed my girl's wrist, practically pulling her with me.

"Hey!" Her mother yelled as if she didn't want us to turn our backs on her, but I didn't give a damn.

Billie quickly grabbed her purse from the table before we left the restaurant. I asked for our plates to be brought up to my room, thus avoiding a fight between mother and daughter.

"Where are we going?" Billie looked breathless, almost running after me.

I realized what I was doing with the girl, slowing down my pace to let her keep up with me.

"To my room," I said quickly.

"To your room?" She frowned in a funny way.

"Yes," I agreed, stopping in front of the elevator.

"Look, I really want to thank you for getting me out of that situation, but did you really need to drag me like a dog?" She rolled her eyes, pulling her hand away from mine.

"I don't have patience for irritating women." I stepped into the elevator with Billie following.

"Well, I hope I don't test your patience then. I can be quite irritating." From the corner of my eye, I saw a mischievous smile forming on her face.

"Believe it or not, your irritating side energizes me," I murmured, turning and cupping her face with both hands, pushing her body roughly against the wall and taking her lips with mine.

I positioned her, opening my mouth and sliding my tongue into hers, savoring the delicious sensation of the kiss.

Her sweet taste, those full lips, I was so excited I could have swallowed her whole.

The sound of the elevator doors opening made me stop, pulling my face quickly away from hers. I looked toward the opening, noticing two men staring at us, clearly embarrassed, but ignoring their looks, I held Billie's wrist and pulled her with me again.

We left, feeling her pull her arm away, clearly hating being taken like this again.

"Damn it, hairy Italian, do you always have to drag me by the wrist?" she complained, following a little behind as I let go of her arm.

"Always is a strong word, considering this is only the second time," I said, stopping in front of the door, typing in the code and seeing it unlock.

I let Billie go in first and followed her right after.

"Can we make a deal?" she asked, walking over to the bed, sitting on it, and crossing her legs, deliberately doing so to make me notice how delicious she looked.

"Depends." I shrugged.

"Let's just have sex tonight. I need to clear up how last night went, without getting attached, without involving feelings—just sex, and tomorrow we go our separate ways."

I started unbuttoning the top of my shirt; at least it seemed like a no-strings-attached kind of deal.

"No awkwardness if we run into each other in Sicily?" I asked, leaving the buttons undone halfway.

"None, like two complete strangers. What happens in Las Vegas stays in Las Vegas." Billie slid her hand down her legs, a move that caught my attention.

After a long day, we found out who was behind the blackmail, with all the data on Martilho Gutiérez, along with our detective who got all his records. I left some of our men watching the Mexican's house; he was sorely mistaken if he thought he had everything under control.

All I wanted at that moment was to have the "Barbie" naked and begging for my touch.

"So, you want to be fucked again?" My voice came out low as I walked toward her.

"We both know you want it too." She bit the corner of her lip.

"Absolutely, I never say no to a good fuck." I crouched down, facing Billie. "I'm not quite sure how our last sex went, but I like to go at it hard..."

I whispered, brushing my lips against hers, biting her lip.

"From the soreness, I don't doubt it." Billie spread her legs, making room for me between them.

"Sore?" I asked, not taking my eyes off hers, starting to get worried.

"That delicious post-sex ache." Her hand held onto the waistband of my pants.

"Ache?" I whispered, confused.

"Nothing major, just the kind of soreness you feel when the sex was wild." She tried to kiss my lips, but a knock on the door made me pull away.

"Our food has arrived," I said, heading toward the door.

"I'm starving." Before opening the door, I glanced at the woman sitting on my bed, who was crossing her legs again.

Fuck! There was something about Billie that turned me on so much. I couldn't tell if it was all the crazy energy around her or just a sudden lust.

CHAPTER NINE

Billie

Matteo's room was bigger than mine, with even a table where we had dinner. I didn't eat much, not wanting to feel stuffed.

I constantly caught the Italian looking at me as if he were coveting what he might get for dessert. I shouldn't be naïve; I admitted I was dying to be in that man's arms.

"Where do you live?" That was the first personal question he asked.

"I have an apartment in Manhattan, but I'm not sure if I'll settle there. Actually, I don't know where I'm going." I shrugged; it wasn't news.

"And you say that so calmly?" he asked, furrowing his brow.

"It's like I'm used to it." I casually stood up from my chair, satisfied, and walked around the table.

Matteo dragged his chair back, creating the opportunity for me to sit on his lap. I wasn't pretending to be a puritan; I liked rough, unapologetic sex.

Sliding my foot along his legs, I mounted his lap, our eyes locked on each other.

"I don't know why, but it worries me that you're like this, lost in the world." His hand tightened around my waist, pulling the fabric of my dress.

"I see myself more as a nomad," I teased, sliding my hands along his neck.

"Don't you like having a place that's just yours, where you know you belong?"

"I don't know what that is, so I can't say whether I like it or not." His chest was nearly bare, with only half of the buttons fastened.

"From my point of view, that's madness." He lifted my dress and, pulling it over my arms, tossed the fabric to the floor.

I was braless, and the cool temperature of the room made me shiver slightly, causing my nipples to harden.

"You're too delicious, Billie." The Italian's eyes traveled down my body; I liked the way he looked at me, as if he were adoring me.

"I'm at a disadvantage." I bit my lip, touching the buttons of his shirt, starting to unfasten them. Matteo helped remove the shirt, revealing his smooth, hairless, tanned chest, with many defined muscles from working out.

I felt him wrapping his fingers around the sides of my panties, and with a single pull, he tore the fragile fabric.

"Now this is better," he murmured with a rough voice, tossing the fabric of my panties to the floor.

Before I had a chance to react, Matteo grabbed me by the waist and lifted me. I stood up without taking off my heels, and he spun me around, positioning me facing the table. Even while seated, he seemed almost at my height. Running his hand down my back, he made me bend over the table where we had been dining.

"Ah, how I wish I could see that ass sticking up for me," he growled, making me let out a yelp as he slapped it. "This is for turning around that night and showing everyone your panties." I gasped as he delivered another slap. "And this is for getting so drunk that you didn't remember our sex..."

"You don't remember either." I smiled with my face pressed against the table. Even though he slapped me hard, it didn't cause me pain, but rather a mix of pleasure and pain.

"I'm a man, a big man; no one could take advantage of me even when drunk, unlike you, who are small, beautiful, and delicate." The Italian brought his face closer to my ass and bit it.

"Ah!" I screamed when he bit down hard; the pain was sharp, making me even more breathless.

"Did it hurt, Billie? Did it hurt?" he asked, feeling his tongue glide over the spot he had bitten.

"Yes... it hurt a lot," I whined.

"Are you feeling the frustration I felt?" He squeezed my ass tightly.

"Yes, oh... yes." I closed my eyes as the Italian placed his face between my cheeks, running his tongue there.

"You're so delicious it's almost cruel to all the other women in the world." I arched my back further, his fingers teasing my pussy.

"Ah, Matteo," I whispered, biting my lip.

The Italian's wet tongue began to slide over my entire ass, even exploring the area that had never been touched by any man before. He had no shame; he was a rough man.

His legs moved closer to me as he dragged the chair nearer.

"Has anyone ever fucked your ass?" he asked, not lifting his face from my butt.

"No..."

"I want to fuck it; I love asses." My eyes widened as I felt the pressure of one of his fingers penetrating me there.

"Ah!" I screamed again.

"If you keep screaming like that, they'll think I'm beating you," he whispered, pulling out his finger and then inserting it again.

"What are you doing, rough Italian?" I grumbled, curious and enjoying it.

"I'm going to suck your pussy dry, until I have every last drop of pleasure in my mouth, without removing my finger from your ass, so you'll remember the only man who made you cum like a madwoman." His face descended between my legs.

I spread my legs, giving him more access to my pussy, leaving it completely at his mercy.

I had always been wild in bed, but I admit Matteo was the first man who could make me feel so vulnerable during sex.

His tongue took over my pussy, my ass arched for him, and unable to contain myself, I began to grind on his face. I wanted everything, a sensation that he might be tearing me apart, his finger slowly entering and exiting my ass; he had big fingers.

Could it be that sensation driving me so wild?

With his other hand, he worked two fingers inside my pussy, licking my folds, letting my moans escape wildly from my mouth. I was at the peak of my pleasure, unable to control all my instincts, wanting everything from him, wanting to give myself up completely.

"Oh, Matteo..." I whimpered.

"Cum, ragazza perfetta, cum..." Hearing him speak in Italian was like touching paradise.

That was the climax; I whimpered and surrendered completely to him, as I had an exhilarating orgasm, falling freely while Matteo sucked me hard, wanting to drain every last drop of pleasure from me.

CHAPTER TEN

Matteo

Without giving her a chance to recover from that orgasm, I turned Billie to face me, sliding my hand under her ass and lifting her up onto my lap, her legs wrapping around my waist.

"What are you going to do now, Italian?" The way she called me Italian was unique to her; no one had called me that before, perhaps because I'd never been involved with an American woman.

"Fuck your pussy." I easily laid the blonde down in the middle of the bed.

My eyes fixed on Billie's delicious body lying in the center of the bed, her long hair spread out.

She propped herself up on her arms, spread her legs, sitting close to the edge of the bed where I was. I grabbed the waistband of my pants, undid the button, and lowered the zipper before sliding them down. She lifted her beautiful blue eyes toward me.

"You know, Italian, the next day I felt like I'd been fucked by a rock, that delicious post-sex soreness. So, I need to see with my own eyes and make sure it's what I'm expecting." Billie easily lowered my pants.

My cock popped out over the waistband of my underwear, practically begging for attention as Billie pulled down my pants, leaving me without shoes. Then, she turned her gaze to my underwear, and I caught a glimpse of her biting the corner of her lip.

"Wow..." was all she said as she pulled down my underwear, dragging one leg against the other as I took off my briefs.

"Suck my cock," I growled, grabbing her hair and holding it in a ponytail.

"I love how rough you are." With a mischievous smile, Billie stuck out her tongue and ran it over the head of my cock. "Some guys with big cocks don't know how to use them. Do you, Matteo?"

She was being provocative, even during sex, the girl liked to tease.

"I know how to shove it down your throat and make you swallow all my cum." I pressed her mouth against my cock, catching her off guard, making her swallow my cock all at once as I heard Billie gag.

At first, Billie coughed, but it didn't make her flinch, holding the base of my cock. She knew what she was doing; her delicate fingers contrasted with the rigid skin of my penis.

"I'm going to suck your cock so good that you'll never forget the one woman who gave you the best blowjob." Billie didn't look away from me, with lust rubbing my cock against her face.

She wanted to repeat what I'd said, and damn, that perfect face around my cock made all other women in the world seem insignificant compared to Billie Harris.

She started sucking the head slowly, going down as far as she could, gagging a few times. My hand around her hair tightened as I was intoxicated by that wonderful sensation.

"Fucking tasty mouth," I roared, keeping my eyes locked on her.

Billie pulled back, stuck out her tongue, and ran it all over my cock, making it look like a juicy lollipop, a popsicle she licked until the end.

Lowering her face, she grabbed my balls, and I felt the exact moment she sucked them with force, in the right place, making me growl from the bottom of my throat. Without stopping, she sucked them, stimulating my cock with her hand; her fingers were so small they barely circled my penis.

"Fuck!!!" I roared again.

"Are you going to spill your cum on my face, or do you want me to swallow it all? I usually don't swallow..."

"Just for that, you're going to take all my cum," I grunted, watching her go back to taking me in her mouth.

Without stopping, she continued to stimulate my balls, taking my entire length into her mouth, or at least as much as she could. I couldn't take it anymore; I wanted everything inside her. I held her hair tightly and started thrusting my cock deeper and deeper into her mouth.

Billie's eyes started tearing up, drool dripped from her mouth, while her plump lips circled my cock.

"In that case, your prayers will be answered." I tilted my head back, roaring like a caveman.

I knew that woman could be my downfall, just as I knew my cock might become demanding after that blowjob.

Pops escaped from Billie's mouth; she never asked me to stop. On the contrary, she seemed to enjoy seeing me vulnerable, being in control of the situation.

Her perfect face, the tears streaming down, our eyes locked, was all it took to push her mouth down to the base of my cock. I came deep in her throat, holding her there, spasms running through my body as I came with force and aggression.

Billie swallowed everything, even choking a bit; she didn't spit out a single drop. I pulled my cock from her mouth, bent down, and pushed her back, my body pressed against hers, my lips taking hers aggressively.

My taste in her mouth, her taste in mine. An urgent kiss, teeth clashing, our tongues sliding over each other, her leg spreading and wrapping around my back.

"Do you use any contraception?" I asked, feeling the urgency to fuck that pussy.

"Yes, but I'm not sure about the effectiveness of the birth control shot I take. It's better if we use a condom. You know, I'm not ready to be a mother." Her fingers traced my back, and I felt the scratch of her nails.

"I'm not the type who aims for a family and kids. I don't even want to be a father; I have too many traumas to want a family," I grunted, getting up from the bed, seeing her look at me with those confused eyes.

I picked up my pants from the floor, knowing that inside my wallet, I always kept two condoms.

"Even though it's not my business, could you tell me why? After all, I just gave you a hell of a blowjob." My eyes met hers as I took out a condom and left the other on the bed in case it was needed.

"You're right, it's none of your business. But don't be upset about it; it's not a topic I like to discuss." I easily put on the condom.

"Fortunately, this will be our last time together because I hate people who don't tell me about their lives." Billie sat on the bed, pouting like a spoiled girl, lifting her hands to run them through my hair. "Now fuck me, rough Italian..."

"Your wish is my command."

CHAPTER ELEVEN

Billie

Matteo covered my body with his, holding my wrists and bringing them above my head. His face was close to mine, and his hair had come loose from the elastic, giving me a view of the man who looked more like a lion with all that wild hair.

My leg wrapped around his body, giving him the opportunity to penetrate me with lust, feeling him press his cock against my entrance.

I bit the corner of my lip. Matteo had a large cock, just like everything about him. His lips descended towards mine, kissing me—a slow, soft, and wet kiss.

Our tongues sliding over each other.

"Let go of my hands," I whimpered in the middle of the kiss.

With a brief smile amidst our act, he released them, giving me the chance to touch his back, sliding my nails over him, feeling that virile man right there on top of me.

The Italian began to penetrate me more forcefully, taking me roughly, as if he knew I had adjusted to his size. He lowered his hand to the back of my neck, gripping it tightly, our eyes locked, the kiss ceased, our noses touching.

"I want to ride you, big guy..." My voice faded, holding that tone of mischief.

"Always with a nickname on the tip of your tongue," he whispered, thrusting slowly inside me.

"I love giving you nicknames, hairy Italian." I let my hand slide down to touch his beard. For a brief moment, I saw him close his eyes and sigh at my touch, but it was brief, as he quickly recovered.

"So ride my cock and show me if Barbies know how to ride," he said with a hint of malice in his voice.

Matteo moved, pulling his cock out of me, lying down beside me. I shifted, placing a leg on each side of his chest and sliding my pussy onto his cock.

"I wish I could be fucking you without this damn condom," he growled, squeezing my waist.

"Unless you're willing to be a daddy, we shouldn't do that." I bit the corner of my lip. "Which reminds me, if we had sex protected that night..."

"I found a used condom beside the bed." He slid his hand down my stomach, caressing it as his fingers traveled. "What a perfect pussy..."

Slowly, I descended onto his cock, feeling him fill me, complete me, my hand pressed against his broad chest.

I loved being on top, having the view of Matteo, his masculine expression, how he tensed up.

Without him removing his fingers from my pussy, stimulating me, I moved up and down on his member, giving small gyrations.

My sweaty hair fell beside my face. With his other hand free, Matteo spread one side of my hair and wrapped it around his hand until it reached the center of my head.

With a pull, he made me bend down, our faces close, a mischievous smile forming on my lips, not stopping my gyrations on his cock.

"I love how rough you are," I repeated, my mouth close to his, biting his lower lip.

"Do you like being treated like a naughty girl?" he asked, moving his hips and penetrating me with more force.

"Oh..." I moaned loudly. "I love being treated like a naughty girl..."

I grabbed his shoulder, my chest close to his. Matteo removed his hand from my pussy, moving it to one of my breasts, dragging his thumb over my hard nipples.

The excitement drove me crazy with pleasure, our lips meeting again in a voracious and hot kiss. In that position, it was easier to move, gyrating faster.

Matteo's sighs grew longer, my moans being taken by his lips.

I was completely surrendered, eagerly desiring the orgasm that was building inside me.

"Oh... Matteo..." I whimpered, gyrating without stopping, going in and out.

The Italian realized I was about to come, so he began to stimulate his cock with more force inside my pussy.

I let out a squeal, surrendering, my body collapsing against his with a high-pitched roar. He also surrendered, one of his hands gripping my hair tightly as the other traveled down my back, pressing me as if he wanted to join us.

Only our heavy breaths echoed in the room, both of us exhausted and spent. I slid my languid fingers through his silky hair and slowly closed my eyes.

"Billie?" he called me.

"Hmm..." I whispered, sliding off him and lying down beside him.

I closed my eyes, hearing his footsteps around the room. I turned my face, opening my eyes to see him running his hand through his hair in a sensual way. He was naked, and his cock didn't seem to have softened; it was still erect as if ready for another round.

"Are you going to tell me you're ready for the next one?" I ran my hand under my head, propping it up on my arm.

"Are you already tired?" The Italian seemed amused by my astonishment.

Matteo stopped beside the bed, bending down, holding my shoulder, and making me lie on my back, his body covering mine.

"I'm still not satisfied with you." He moved his face down, leaving kisses on my neck. "We have another condom..."

"Do you want to use it?" I closed my eyes, intoxicated by the moment.

"Yes..." His lips moved down to the center of my breasts, pinching the tip of a nipple.

"Oh..." I let out a squeal as he began to lick the nipple.

He seemed insatiable, wanting to get me ready for him again.

"Deliziosa could easily become my favorite drug," he groaned as with his other hand he took hold of my pussy, fingering it with his fingers.

Without stopping sucking on my nipples, he alternated between them, squeezing them with his hand as he flicked his tongue on one. I raised my hand and dragged it across the Italian's back.

Everything about him was extremely pleasurable, his masculine scent, the rough yet delicate way he took me—it was as if Matteo could tame both versions.

I felt completely ready for that Italian again, my pussy dripping like honey.

"Oh, big guy, take me as yours again," I whimpered, his fingers getting lost in my honey.

"Don't ask twice," he growled, biting the tip of my nipple hard.

"You bastard." I wanted to slap him, but I ended up reaching for the condom instead.

CHAPTER TWELVE

Matteo

The blonde's hair sprawled beside me revealed that I had succumbed to temptation, and there was the spoiled girl I swore I wouldn't fuck again. What the hell was she doing on my sheets? How was Billie Harris, for the second time, sleeping in the same bed as me?

I didn't repeat women; the last one I did that with ended up being my girlfriend, and she demanded more than she should have from me, a marriage that was never on the table.

She wanted marriage, a happy family—something I had been stalling on, making her believe that someday she would get what she always wanted. I loved Juliana, but she left me for someone who could offer what I never could: marriage, a family, children.

My phone buzzed beside the bed. I picked it up, seeing Valentino's name flashing on the screen. I walked to the balcony door, opening it in just my underwear, looking out over the city that never slept, Las Vegas.

"Let's act," he said quickly.

"Act?" I ran a hand through my hair, pushing it back.

"I talked to my wife; she's willing to take the risk. I want you to organize the best men in Las Vegas, and go into Martilho's house. Leave only when everyone is dead, including Martilho Gutiérez," the Don spoke with conviction.

"By your tone, I don't need to ask if you're sure," I whispered thoughtfully.

52

"My friend, just do your best. I don't want my wife's video circulating anywhere; I need to take this risk," he sighed heavily.

There was a video of Valentino with his wife, recorded secretly during a sexual act. The *Don* was being blackmailed: either he left Las Vegas, or Martilho, who was behind it all, would release the video online.

"That was the most sensible choice, Don." I had already given that alternative to Valentino.

But apparently, all he needed was his wife's green light. I always knew Valentino wouldn't be an unfaithful husband, no matter what he said. I knew well the Italian who led that mafia, seeing the reflection of all the men in that family. The *Don* would be the next to fall in love. And I didn't judge him; I had fallen in love myself and chose to let her go because I could never give her what she wanted.

We ended the call, and before going back into the room, I texted Mike, asking him to gather everyone at the club. I needed all the Cosa Nostra soldiers, all the *Caporegimes*, not missing a single one.

Mike was in charge of everything there; when no high-ranking Cosa Nostra members were present, he was the one in command.

I entered the room, seeing the curvaceous woman sitting on the bed, running her hand through her long blonde hair. I didn't know much about women's hair color; I just liked it long enough to grab and pull.

"Stupid, stupid, stupid..." The girl kept repeating without noticing my presence. "Billie, where have you ended up..."

"I'd be offended if you didn't remember, after all, you weren't drunk," I cut in, seeing her clear eyes meet mine, her slightly plump lips parting in a soft "oh."

That was the second time we ended up in the same bed, and I didn't even know how it happened the first time.

And here we were again, a second time, with sex that we both remembered—the first time didn't count. Even though I knew it was her, I didn't recall the details of her body from that first time. Did this make it the first time?

"I thought you had already left." Billie brought her finger to her mouth, the same finger I had sucked the night before, those pink nails sliding across my chest.

"I'm leaving now," I said, finding my pants on the floor, going to her and picking them up.

"You remembered everything from last night, didn't you?"

"Yes," I answered without looking at her, putting on my pants.

"Then we don't need to repeat it; we've both satisfied our curiosity." I raised my eyes as she wandered casually around the room.

Billie wasn't shy about exposing her body, and damn, she didn't need to be; she was the kind of woman who caught my eye. Perfectly shaped to be held in my arms and even turned inside out.

She had that small jewel in her navel, the pointed breasts that she had just dressed with her dress.

"Where's your underwear?" I asked, noticing that the girl was wearing the dress without any panties.

"Do you really think I'm going to wear underwear that was left on a hotel floor, possibly harboring bacteria and diseases? I'd rather go without. Besides, I don't know if you remember, but you tore it," she shrugged.

"But you're in a dress. If you spread your legs a bit more, you could reveal your intimacy." I didn't know why that bothered me.

"What does it matter? I showed you just now, and nothing happened," she was nonchalant.

Billie gathered her hair into a bun on top of her head, her eyes meeting mine.

"Well, I'm heading back to New York today. My curiosity is satisfied. I hope I met your expectations." She picked up her heel and put it on.

"I feel the same way," I said, and her eyes dropped to my abdomen.

"I've been with better," she said with a slight shrug.

"I'd never claim to be the best," I mocked, watching her bite the tip of her lip.

"You got it right, hairy Italian." The woman winked at me.

Without even coming over to say goodbye, she headed for the door, grabbed the handle, but turned before leaving.

"You know, Matteo, you're really good in bed. You just need to accept that, for the first time in your life, you came like a little boy." She pouted in a self-satisfied manner.

"Seriously? What makes you say that?"

"Men like you don't let women take charge. I had you, and you came like a kid. It's a shame, knowing we'll never repeat this." Billie didn't wait for my reply, opened the door, and left.

We weren't going to repeat it. I didn't repeat women; it was an easy way to avoid the risk of falling in love.

I let out a long sigh, finishing getting dressed. I needed to get started on Valentino's plan.

CHAPTER THIRTEEN

Matteo

The moment of tension left me anxious. Breaking into Martilho's house was easier than we had expected; they were caught off guard. There was no effective protection for the leader of that small gang. They were new and completely unprepared. The house turned into a river of blood, demonstrating the consequences for anyone who thought they could mess with the Cosa Nostra.

My eyes were fixed on the computer, Martilho's lifeless body sprawled on the floor next to me, having been shot by one of my men. The bastard knew we were there, that the Cosa Nostra's men were coming in, knew he couldn't escape, and put his plan into action.

It was like a ticking time bomb, the video loading, ready to be uploaded to the internet at any moment.

Next to me, my phone was on a video call, receiving instructions from our clan's hacker. I didn't know much about that kind of technology, but I followed his directions carefully.

I hated all the tension, hated knowing that the Don's fate was in my hands.

"Go to the permissions settings, click cancel, it's in the top tab of the computer," the hacker instructed, and I did as told.

I had been in so many places that I hadn't even paid attention to how I got to that tab. I found the cancel option. I received the following message: "Upload canceled."

"Fuck, I did it," I swore loudly, relieved that it was over.

"Now can someone explain what happened?" Valentino asked as I picked up my phone, showing my face, and seeing the Don's face on the screen.

"We won, Don. Las Vegas is ours, and the video is no longer scheduled." I leaned back in the chair, even managing a smile amidst my relief.

"What do you mean?" The Don wanted the details since we hadn't had a chance to talk since the attack began.

Valentino had returned to Sicily earlier, interrupting even his honeymoon. He needed to be there because we had traitors infiltrated within our ranks, right inside our headquarters.

"We broke into Martilho's house; he definitely didn't expect it. We arrived shooting everyone, and when we reached him, the man clearly didn't know how to use the computer and we had already killed his IT guy. The video was scheduled to be released at 11:59 PM. Martilho tried to upload it earlier but didn't know how, and in desperation, started smashing the computers. But as you can see, not everything was broken, and we caught him unarmed. It was easier than we expected. We killed everyone; nothing was left. This is Cosa Nostra, damn it!" I ran my hand through my hair, pushing it back. In the midst of all that chaos, I must have lost my tie somewhere.

Valentino disconnected the call and handed the phone back to the hacker, who gave me a few final instructions to completely delete the video.

When we finished, I got up from the chair, grabbed the gun from my back, and aimed it at the shattered computers, firing non-stop, demolishing everything, leaving not a single piece behind.

"Consigliere?" I raised my face as I put away my gun.

"We need to leave," I said, knowing what the soldier would say, watching him nod.

I looked down at the body of the bastard lying on the floor, knowing it was proof of what happens to those who mess with us. I ran my hand over my face, and then noticed the blood on my fingers. Great, I had blood on my face.

I didn't worry about it at that moment, just directed my men.

"I want our crest left behind. They need to know that this work of art was done by the Cosa Nostra. That way, no fool will want to mess with our clan." Decided, I left the room.

I dodged the bodies on the floor, walking through the corridors. There must have been about 12 dead men, all unprepared, with no idea of what it meant to be there.

I reached outside the residence, finding our cars. A door was opened for me. I approached, taking the towel that was handed to me.

"Let's go to the hotel," I ordered as I got into the car. "I'm going to pack my bag and head back to Sicily. I have nothing else to do here."

I liked my home, the comfort that only my place could provide me. I had been away from the solitude of my room for too long.

Our nightclub in Las Vegas was once again secure, under our control, with no jokers able to take it over.

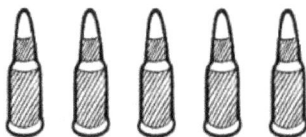

I ENTERED THE HOTEL, aware of my deplorable state, but at least the blood had been washed off, so I didn't look like I had just come from a small war.

I let out a long sigh, stopping in front of the elevator. I had already messaged my *caporegime* to get the jet ready. I hadn't brought many men with me from Sicily since we had plenty of soldiers and *caporegimes* at our disposal here, loyal men working in Las Vegas.

The doors opened. Taking a step back, I wanted to let people exit, but my eyes met hers—the crazy blonde. She was carrying a pink rolling suitcase, as if I should expect anything different from her.

Our eyes locked. She came toward me, sighing again. I knew she was going to say something to me, but I wasn't sure if we should talk.

"Wow, you look like you've been run over," she said, speaking casually.

"Just your impression," I declared coldly, as I always did with women after sex.

"Damn, what did I do to make you so cold?" she asked, frowning.

"Didn't we have an agreement? Why are you talking to me?" I didn't want to be so arrogant with her, but I had to. I didn't want Billie to think we had a friendship when we didn't. I didn't have female friends; they were just for sex.

"Yes, we did, but I thought that—"

"You thought wrong. No contact, no conversation, no eye contact. I don't like the type of woman you are." My eyes traveled down her body. She was beautiful, even in a short dress. Billie would never stop being beautiful.

"What are you trying to say?" Without any pretense, she wanted to know.

"You're vulgar." I curled my lip, hating myself inside. I wasn't one to do that sort of thing, but we had mutual acquaintances, and I didn't want her to think we could stay in touch every time she was in Sicily.

"Vulgar?" Billie's eyes widened. "You're such a jerk. Go back to your miserable life in Sicily. I hope you cry acid tears over your ex, she's what you deserve after you left her. What an arrogant bastard!!!"

She turned, taking her suitcase with her. I got what I wanted, just as I always did with women, but I didn't know why this time it was hard, like something was squeezing inside me. I didn't want to have treated Billie that way, but it was necessary.

At least that's what I wanted to convince myself.

CHAPTER FOURTEEN

Billie

Five months later...

"How long are you going to hide this pregnancy?" Yulia asked anxiously on the other end of the line, always wanting me to leave my apartment.

"Until she's born?" I asked, sitting on my sofa after a yoga class.

"Girl, I can't stand being away from you. Come visit me," Yulia kept insisting, and I admit I was almost giving in.

"If I go, he'll find out about the pregnancy," my voice came out weak, filled with fear.

"Matteo doesn't even mention your name anymore, friend," she said, knowing I didn't want to see that big jerk in front of me either.

"He called me vulgar, he might even think this baby is from someone else," I murmured, lost in thought.

I admitted I wanted to leave that apartment. I was tired of seeing those same walls all the time. It felt like my life had stopped. I didn't want to work anymore, and I even gave up the project I was doing with a modeling school.

My parents had definitely abandoned me after they found out about the pregnancy, having the audacity to say they didn't want any more ties with me, that the pregnancy could damage their image, since I became a single mother.

Taking that home pregnancy test and seeing the positive result felt like opening a hole and throwing myself into it. At first, I felt confused and lost; I couldn't even take care of myself, let alone a child.

"Friend, come to Sicily. Let's go through our pregnancy together. We can even work together," Yulia said, pulling me out of my reverie.

"That offer is tempting," I declared.

"You'll like it here. You won't be alone," Yulia kept insisting.

"You're right, it's lonely here. I'm afraid to go out, afraid of someone photographing me and turning it into some sensational news, all because I'm the daughter of those two." I rolled my eyes.

I wasn't famous like my parents; in fact, I didn't even consider myself a person of fame. But when journalists wanted to hit those two, they came after the weakest link, which was me, since I never liked anything in that world, and ended up in various news stories—my parents' worst nightmare.

"So, come on, friend," Yulia pleaded again.

"Alright, you win. You've convinced me with your persistence. But promise me one thing?" I asked, looking at my rounded belly, knowing my little baby was inside.

"I promise."

"I don't want Matteo to know this baby is his. If it were up to me, he'd never find out," I said firmly.

"But friend, that's selfish. He needs to know. And what if someday your daughter wants to know who her father is?"

"I'll say he died in a car accident. My little angel won't know what it's like to be snubbed by someone. She doesn't need to know she has a father who never wanted her, who made it clear he never intended to have children. Growing up as the rejected daughter gave me enough reason to not want the same for my daughter," I had that answer on the tip of my tongue.

Once the shock of discovering the pregnancy passed, positive thoughts began to emerge about everything I could do as a mother.

I had always wanted to be a mother, though I didn't want it at that moment. But it happened, and growing inside me was my little thing. Discovering her gender was enough to confirm that I wanted to make my daughter's life a bed of roses. Everything I didn't have, I wanted to give her, showering her with love and affection, making her feel like the only one in the world. It would be just me and her against the world.

"So can I count on your arrival?" My friend sounded hopeful.

"Yes, it seems like deep down, you won. I'm coming," I declared, hearing Yulia's excited squeal.

We ended the call after finalizing everything about the trip. Yulia wanted to ask one of her family's jets to pick me up, but I didn't want that. I preferred to fly commercially, close to other people. But first, I needed to talk to my obstetrician about the trip.

I got up from the sofa, my belly at a medium size, I could say I was past the halfway mark of my pregnancy. I caressed the protruding bulge, loving the sensation of feeling her little kicks.

They said that over time, the kicks would become uncomfortable, but there was nothing about that little one that made me more enchanted. Discovering the pregnancy was like flipping a switch inside me. I wanted that baby with all my heart and would do anything for her.

I went into the kitchen, grabbed a glass from the rack, and filled it with water, taking small sips.

After my encounter with Matteo at the hotel, where he was a complete jerk with me for no reason, I just wanted to talk to him, to understand why he was acting that way, so disheveled. I worried about him, and all I got was his arrogance.

What hurt the most was being away from my friend, away from Yulia, only talking through calls. She was pregnant too, expecting twins. I wanted to be there, experiencing everything up close, but there was a greater force keeping me away—my little Felicity, the happiness that had come into my life.

When I thought everything might crumble, happiness came into my life.

Everyone could judge me for seeming crazy, having a child with a man who didn't even want to know about me, who clearly stated he didn't want a family. But I was crazy enough to face that world for my daughter.

I knew Felicity was Matteo's child. I might have committed the greatest madness, but I didn't usually sleep with men regularly. It was one every month, and sometimes even that didn't happen.

With Matteo, there was that one time, the time neither of us remembered what happened. And the condom he saw next to his bed, there was no doubt it wasn't our only sexual encounter. We must have done it more than once, which resulted in my pregnancy.

Valentino, Yulia's husband, knew about my pregnancy and also knew his friend well enough not to mention anything about the baby to him. He just told Yulia that he would continue pretending he didn't know anything because it wasn't his problem.

I returned to the living room, grabbed my phone, and called my obstetrician. I needed to make sure everything was okay for the trip.

CHAPTER FIFTEEN

Billie

The plane finally landed on Italian soil. It was time to dust off my Italian language skills.

I didn't land in Sicily but in a neighboring city, so I had to drive to my friend's house. When passengers were finally allowed to disembark, I almost thanked them—or rather, my stomach almost thanked them, as I was feeling very nauseous. I didn't know this could happen, but my obstetrician had warned me before approving my trip.

The truth is, I should have accepted my friend's husband's jet. I wouldn't have had to go through all that discomfort.

I followed the line, walking behind the people. I went down the steps of the small staircase, heading toward the baggage claim. My pink suitcase was easy to spot. First one came, then the other. I grabbed the handles and started pushing them, following the exit signs.

Yulia had said that one of her husband's men would be waiting for me. She even wanted to come herself but didn't want to risk a one-hour car trip to get here, which would be an hour each way.

There was no need for her to come; we would be together soon enough. In fact, I didn't even know when I'd be returning. My obstetrician had only advised me not to delay my return when the pregnancy was more advanced and, if necessary, to have my routine exams done in Sicily, which wasn't a problem since Yulia also had to have hers, and we were almost at the same gestational stage, with only a week difference.

I approached the exit and found a man dressed entirely in black holding a sign with my name. I walked up to him and said:

"That's me, Billie." I pointed to the sign, and he merely nodded, not saying a word or showing a smile, looking almost petrified.

Another man was with him, who took charge of my suitcase while they guided me to the exit, where three black cars were waiting. Did they really need all that just to pick me up? *What a madness*, I even felt like a queen.

They loaded my bags into the trunk. Soon, the car started moving. I focused my attention on the window, admiring the beautiful landscapes. The place was so stunning it left me almost breathless.

I took out my phone and sent a message to Yulia, letting her know I'd be arriving soon.

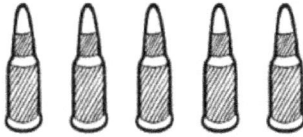

I KEPT MY EYES OPEN throughout the journey, amazed, loving being there for the second time, the first being at Yulia's wedding.

A wedding that started out of convenience, which I thought was completely crazy, but apparently, it was normal among mafia families. I should have been scared, I shouldn't have been there, since I was staying at the residence of criminals.

The father of my child was a criminal, *wow*! I had never thought about that. Did Felicity, my little happiness, have mafia blood?

I noticed the car slowing down, passing through a huge gate—it was the gated community where my friend lived with her husband's family.

As soon as we reached the beginning of the street, the car stopped in front of a luxurious house, possibly the largest in the area.

Before I even had time to open the door, one of those men had already done it, extending his hand to me. I stepped out and stopped in front of the sidewalk, taking a deep breath and smelling the faint scent of the sea in the distance.

The last time I was in that same place, I loved the delicious freshness, the way I could hear the sound of the sea if I went to the end of the property. It was all so beautiful, so magical.

I lifted my face and saw the door of the house open. It was late afternoon, the sun was setting in the distance, and I focused on the open door and my friend walking through it.

If I thought my belly was big, Yulia's seemed twice the size.

"Friend!" She squealed, hurrying toward me.

I did the same, stopping in front of her. We hugged awkwardly, unable to contain my tears of joy. If there was one thing that pregnancy had done, it was make my hormones very sensitive, and crying had never been so easy.

"Wow, I've missed you so much." I sniffed as I pulled away after we had been hugging for a long time.

"Can I tie you to the foot of the table so you never leave?" she asked with a playful tone, holding my fingers and leading me toward the entrance.

"I feel like I'm home. The smell of this place wins me over," I declared as I walked through the door, hearing voices coming from inside the house.

"Maybe that's a sign," Yulia glanced back over her shoulder at me.

"Only if it's a sign for me to run away," I joked, rolling my eyes.

Yulia was the first to enter the living room, while my eyes scanned the people who were there— they were all women.

"Billie, this is my mother-in-law Verena, my two sisters-in-law Pietra and Cinzia," she said, pointing to the women present. It was amazing how young my friend's mother-in-law looked; she was beautiful, seeming like a delicate woman.

"Look, we have another pregnant woman," said the blonde woman, placing her hand on her very large belly, which looked like it was about to pop any moment.

"I don't know how good that can be," the other sister-in-law said. She was Yulia's husband's sister, while Cinzia, the other one, was the wife of Yulia's other brother. "Too many hormones together—keep them away from me. I don't want more kids..."

"Did you forget that your husband had a vasectomy?" The mother-in-law said, looking mockingly at her daughter Pietra.

"With so many hormones, it might fail," the woman made a funny face.

I remembered them very well from when I was here last time. It was impossible to forget such beautiful and hospitable women.

"It's good to have you here, Billie. Yulia kept complaining that her friend was far away and didn't want to visit her," Mrs. Verena said, looking at her daughter-in-law with affection.

"I can only imagine the drama she made," I smiled to the side as I heard footsteps coming from the stairs and turned my neck to see the three men coming down.

"I was almost going to fetch you myself," I knew that was Yulia's husband; he had a twin brother. "Anything to make my wife happy."

Sensually, I saw him wink at Yulia. Even though they might have married under strange circumstances, it was clear how much they loved each other now.

"I wouldn't doubt it..." My sentence trailed off as my eyes fixed on the last man to come down the stairs.

Our eyes met briefly, but he quickly looked away as if I were nothing, as if we had never been involved in the past.

I was good at hiding my feelings and put on my best smile. Maybe I had inherited that acting skill from my parents.

"I'll be going now. We'll talk via message," his voice was like a balm to my ears.

But Matteo completely ignored me; he didn't even look at me properly. Yulia must have been right—he didn't care about anything regarding me.

CHAPTER SIXTEEN

Matteo

I left the house, exhaling a breath I hadn't even realized I was holding. Fuck!

What was that all about? Why did I act that way?

It was easy to pretend that the crazy woman didn't exist when she was far away, but seeing her there, the way our eyes met briefly, I could see the explicit hurt.

I wanted to talk to Billie, ask her if she had moved on with her life, but I didn't. Keeping my distance was better. After all, why should I care about a woman who was nothing to me? It was just a fling like all the others I've had in my life.

I tried to convince myself of that in vain, even speaking out loud. Why the hell did I care about that woman?

There was only one explanation—it was because she was so lonely, so alone that she created the worst situations to get attention.

I blinked several times, pulling a cigarette from my pocket, putting one in my mouth, and walked toward the car door that was open for me. I didn't live in that condominium; they even offered me a house to stay close to my Don, but I ended up declining.

My house wasn't far from the condominium. I could reach the headquarters quickly when necessary, so I chose to continue living where I was.

With the car window open, I continued smoking my cigarette as the car moved out of the condominium.

The headquarters of the Cosa Nostra was in the same residence as the Don's, large enough to accommodate all the men for meetings, and even his family, to live in it.

It wasn't long before the driver stopped in front of my house.

"Be at my disposal if needed," I said, watching him nod.

Our drivers were clan members, trained to kill if necessary. Under no circumstances did we leave without security; all the men of the Cosa Nostra were armed.

I entered my house, heading to the living room, leaving the cigarette butt on the ashtray on the furniture.

I let out a long sigh that could even echo through that silent house.

When I bought it, it was entirely deliberate. I had a fiancée; initially, Juliana thought that with that house, she would change her mind and finally build the family she so longed for. But it was just another one of my strategies to string her along.

I didn't want to let go of Juliana. She was a steady fuck, kind, liked to talk to me, and calm—the type of woman who simply obeyed. But if there was one thing she wanted and wouldn't change her mind about, it was the damn family. For years, I tried to get that out of her head, even proposing marriage with the condition that we wouldn't have children.

Obviously, she refused. Juliana wanted it all, a complete marriage. And she would never have that from me.

I couldn't look at Santino and see myself as a father like him. I couldn't imagine being a good father. My father killed my mother in front of me, mercilessly. It wounded me, hurt deep in my soul, and what if I became a man like him? What if I did the same to some child of mine?

Every time I looked at Juliana, the image of Mom came to mind—the way she was submissive to my father, even with him doing all that to her. Mom loved him, a sick love. They were both sick, so much so that my father never had another relationship after killing his wife, as if he really didn't think when he killed her, only to regret it right after.

I could never accept that as love!

I went to the back of the house, the sea right there, a private beach, with no people on it. The lawn at the back of the property merged with the sand, all the way to the edge of the sea. The pool, which had never been used by anyone, not even Juliana.

It was the view that made me fall in love with that house. From my bedroom, it had a splendid view, a place just for me.

It was supposed to be mine and Juliana's, but within a week of buying the house, she realized that nothing would change. That house was just another of my schemes to try to keep her.

Juliana pressed me; she wanted everything or nothing. And when she saw that I wouldn't give her anything, she left, she left forever.

I believed she might have thought I would go after her, that losing her would make me appreciate what we had, and we would finally get married. But that never happened. Strangely enough, when Juliana left, it felt like a weight was lifted from me. I no longer had that pressure.

I didn't need to fight to have her by my side without marriage. Deep down, maybe I didn't want her anymore.

It was convenient; having her by my side was convenient. And that was almost cowardly of me.

I went back inside my house, looking at the long sofa, everything in light tones, designed the way I asked. Living alone had its advantages, but having a woman by my side was better. But not there. In my house, only those I really knew were allowed.

I turned to the stairs, climbing the steps slowly, unbuttoning my shirt, seeing those blue eyes again in my mind. What was it about Billie? Even when Juliana was gone, I didn't think about her like I did about Billie.

Hell! It must be the lack of sex, but how could I sleep with a woman when all I looked for in them were the qualities that crazy girl had? It was ridiculous. I wasn't a teenager anymore; I was a man, having sex just for pleasure, just to satisfy myself. Why the hell did it need to be different now?

I was getting irritated. I threw my shirt on my impeccably made bed; I had a housekeeper who always kept my place organized. Terry was discreet, did everything, and never showed her face to avoid bothering me.

Again, I was going to take a shower and stimulate myself as if I were a teenager at the height of puberty.

And that was because I couldn't find any woman good enough to fuck, becoming too demanding after Billie Harris crossed my path.

CHAPTER SEVENTEEN

Billie

I woke up earlier than I expected. I thought I had slept too long, but when I checked my phone, which I had set to Italy's time zone, I was surprised to see that it was only seven in the morning.

Slowly, I got out of bed and decided to dress slowly, choosing one of my loose dresses with thin straps, trying as much as possible to keep my cleavage discreet. I wasn't in my own house; I needed to dress modestly since I was in a family home, surrounded by married women and children.

After a long time, I even did my hair, pulling it back with some curls styled with a hairdryer.

I put on my medium heels and left the room. The house was silent as I walked through the corridor, taking one step down at a time. I wasn't walking fast; I hoped to find someone awake.

Yulia, with her pregnancy, was waking up later. According to my friend, she couldn't fall asleep early and ended up going to bed late and waking up late.

I entered the living room and immediately regretted it, seeing several people present, including him, the Italian.

"Hello, dear, did you sleep well?" asked Mrs. Verena.

"Like an angel." I gave a brief smile.

Since Matteo had ignored me the last time he was here, I planned to do the same.

"Um..." I cleared my throat, trying not to be intrusive. "I need some orange juice. Can you direct me to where I can get some?"

I asked Mrs. Verena.

"Yes, of course. Breakfast is already being served." She got up from the sofa.

"Oh, don't worry. The orange juice helps me with my morning sickness, a habit I picked up when I found out I was pregnant."

Saying "pregnancy" out loud near Matteo made me want to look at him and see his reaction, but I stayed strong and didn't look. I wouldn't look!

"Don't worry, dear. I know all about adjusting to pregnancy fluctuations." Verena gestured for me to follow her.

As I turned my face and followed Mrs. Verena, my eyes met Matteo's briefly. His expression clearly showed surprise, but I wasn't going to say anything.

We entered the dining room. The breakfast table was set, and there was a jug of orange juice.

"Yulia told us that you only drink orange juice, so I made sure we had plenty." Mrs. Verena, who was about my height, turned to look at me. "Yulia mentioned your baby's father. Know that you can count on me for anything, even in the art of causing jealousy. I can't believe that man was capable of snubbing you and treating you like that."

"So you know he's the father of my Felicity?" I asked in a whisper, seeing her nod.

"Yes, Matteo is the son of old members of our clan. I know everything about his life. And I also know that man is unyielding. To touch his heart, you have to show that you've moved on, and he hasn't." Mrs. Verena had a mischievous smile on her lips.

"I don't even want to think about that arrogant Italian." I rolled my eyes.

"Are you sure? Not even a little jealousy?"

"I'm pregnant. Who would want anything to do with me?" Mrs. Verena pulled out a chair.

"Let's sit down while we talk." We sat next to each other, making it easier for us to whisper. "Dear, you're beautiful, you're pregnant, not dead. I remember when I was carrying my children; I had an insatiable sex drive."

Verena winked at me.

"Well, let's say I have some great toys," I murmured, not shy about talking about this topic.

"So, men like Matteo de Luca, you get them by showing that he lost out..."

"But he lost his fiancée and didn't even bother to go after her." I pursed my lips, remembering the woman who should be married to someone else.

"Let's say it will be a test. I'll ask one of the mafia men to hit on you. I have some great accomplices here." Verena seemed to be thinking hard, strategizing how to put her plan into action. "If someone hits on you in front of him, we'll know if Matteo feels anything. And if he doesn't..."

At that moment, we were interrupted by the men who entered the dining room.

"I'm going to the office. I'm not hungry; I already had breakfast at home," the mafioso's voice echoed in the room, clearly leaving because of me.

"Alright, soon Valentino will come down and we'll talk about that matter," the man who claimed to be my friend's husband said. It was his twin, Santino.

Santino sat in the chair facing his mother.

"Haven't you eaten at home, dear?" Verena asked her son affectionately.

"Yes, but I never refuse a meal." He took a slice of cake and brought it to his mouth.

"Since you're here, we need your help." I widened my eyes, focusing my attention on Mrs. Verena. "Oh, dear, it's not what you're thinking. Santino is the best at setting up jealousy situations..."

"That's when I'm not the target," he mocked.

"Yes, that's true," they seemed to have a good mother-son dialogue.

"What do you need?" he asked in the plural as if he knew I was involved.

"We want to create a jealousy situation for Matteo, to test how he'll react to seeing another man near Billie." The twin looked at me for a long time.

"Matteo won't react. That man is emotionless. I'm sorry, but don't fall in love with him; he'll break your heart."

"That's what I tried to say," I murmured, looking at Mrs. Verena, who ignored what her son had said.

"No, Santino, I feel he does care about her. I saw the way he looked at her today. We need to test that," Mrs. Verena insisted.

"Alright, if that's what you want, I have the perfect person. He's one of our *caporegimes*, the most notorious of all here. He knows how to hit on a woman and can keep a secret. But I don't think he needs to know this is a jealousy plan. If he finds out it's meant to make Matteo jealous, he won't accept it. No other man would either. Everyone here knows Matteo's short fuse; he kills without considering the consequences. So, I'll just tell him that my sister-in-law's friend is here and is single..."

"But I'm pregnant. How will he be interested in a woman like that?" I asked, confused.

"We're talking about Geovane. He doesn't care whether you're pregnant or not. He'll understand when he sees you. But know this: if Matteo really does care, you'll cause trouble. He'll make Geovane's life hell..."

"It's better not to. I don't like this conversation, especially the way you're talking about Matteo." I shook my head negatively.

"Matteo won't make anyone's life hell; we'll make his life a complete chaos. Let's put this plan into action. You can talk to Geovane; he's ideal for us," Mrs. Verena said in a way that even seemed like she knew this Geovane well.

CHAPTER EIGHTEEN

Matteo

Seeing Billie's prominent belly made me uneasy. I didn't know she was pregnant.

"Did you know?" I asked Valentino as soon as I saw him entering his office.

I always had breakfast with the Vacchianos, but seeing Billie sitting there triggered all my alarm systems, making me retreat to the headquarters office.

"Know what exactly?" he asked nonchalantly.

"About Billie's pregnancy?"

"Oh, that. Yes, I knew." He sat down in his chair behind the desk.

Spending years with the Vacchiano twins made it easy to distinguish them by their mannerisms. Santino was more flamboyant, while Valentino was quieter.

"And why am I apparently the only one who didn't know?" I crossed my legs, directing my gaze at my Don.

"Simple. You said in no uncertain terms that you didn't want to know about her anymore, so I just did what you asked." He opened the drawer next to his desk and took out his cigar box.

"Alright, I'm partly to blame, but I should have known she was pregnant," I persisted.

"Really? But why did you need to know?" Valentino could be quite a pain when he wanted to be.

"What if that child is mine?" I got straight to the point.

"I thought you never had unprotected sex. Aren't you supposed to be the most upright man?"

"So, there's no chance it could be mine?" I admitted I was somewhat desperate for answers and didn't even know how to get them directly from her.

"I don't know. I don't involve myself in other people's lives." The Don didn't even look at me, continuing to prepare his cigar.

"If I didn't know you well enough, I might believe that." I rolled my eyes, getting up from the armchair where I was sitting and moving to the chair in front of the Don's desk.

"Honestly, my friend, I can't tell you. When it comes to my wife's friends, I usually don't get involved. Yulia and I don't always see eye to eye, and since Billie isn't involved in important aspects of our lives, I let Yulia handle it on her own. Now, as for Billie's pregnancy, I'll just say this: she doesn't know who the father of her child is, and I'll be clear—don't go accusing her. If you do, it will affect my pregnant wife, and if it affects her, then it becomes my concern," he finished, placing the cigar in his mouth.

"Great, and I thought my life was calm enough." I leaned my head back, letting out a long sigh.

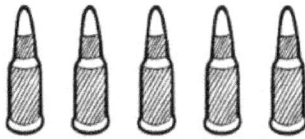

WHEN I LEFT THE OFFICE, it was already past noon. Valentino had stayed with me as we were dealing with issues with the gangs associated with our mafia.

"I'm fucking starving," Valentino grumbled, getting up from his chair.

I just nodded in agreement, and as we passed through the office door, Santino briefly appeared and then left, needing to deal with the *Caporegimes* of the Cosa Nostra.

I went down the stairs right behind the Don.

"Yulia is by the pool. I'm going to talk to her," Valentino said, turning toward the back of the headquarters.

"I'll come with you. I want to smoke a cigarette before we eat," I declared casually.

He nodded in agreement, and we went through the back door of the headquarters, where the pool was located, and just behind it, a few meters away, was the Cosa Nostra hideout where we kept deserters, enemies, and prisoners who had tried to go against the Cosa Nostra at some point.

Valentino went straight to his wife, who was sitting at the edge of the pool under a sunshade. But of course, my traitorous eyes immediately sought her out. I needed to see Billie pregnant, how her body was changing with those curves.

But what I saw made my body tense, my hands clenched into fists, and a cloudy veil covered my eyes.

"Is something wrong, dear?" I heard Valentino's mother's voice from somewhere far off. I couldn't focus on her, only on the sight my eyes couldn't believe.

Billie was lying on a lounge chair, her belly exposed, wearing a bikini that accentuated her small belly. Her breasts seemed too large for that tiny bikini. I quickly recognized the *Caporegime* beside her. *Geovane*!

What the hell was he doing next to my girl? Geovane didn't deserve Billie's smiles, didn't even deserve to be talking to her. Damn it! She was pregnant, what did he want with a pregnant woman?

My blood boiled, anger surged in my mind, and I experienced a feeling I had never felt before—jealousy! I was jealous seeing him there, jealous of seeing Billie return the smile to a man who wasn't me!

I wanted to go over there, blow Geovane's brains out, forgetting that he was a member of our clan, just removing him from the life of a woman who shouldn't belong to anyone.

With just one step, I felt someone grab my arm. From the delicate hands, I knew it was a woman.

"Where do you think you're going?" It was still Valentino's mother beside me, one of the women I respected the most, a motherly figure when mine was taken from me.

Blinking several times, as if trying to return to reality.

"I need to take care of something," was all I said.

"What exactly?" She raised an eyebrow slightly.

What exactly? I repeated the question to myself. Where did I think I was going? What exactly was in my head to go to Billie and remove that man from her side?

"Nothing..." My voice trailed off, looking again at the woman lying on the lounge chair, all my instincts screaming fiercely inside me, *go to our girl and get that piece of shit away from her.*

"Matteo? Is everything okay?" Verena asked again.

"No... I mean yes, everything's perfectly fine," my voice clearly betrayed how lost I was in my thoughts.

"Then why do you keep staring at Yulia's friend?" Great, now I looked like a lunatic.

"Just your imagination." I took a deep breath, regaining control of my body, or at least a little of it, just to get out of there. "I need to go..."

Dodging Verena, practically running with quickened steps and panting, I swore on everything inside me that I was going to punch the hell out of that bastard Geovane for thinking he could hit on a pregnant woman!

CHAPTER NINETEEN

Billie

"What I don't understand is how someone as beautiful as you is alone." That man had a certain charm; his confidence could win over any woman.

"I don't know if you've noticed, but I have a pretty big belly." I gave a brief smile as I sat in the lounger.

"Pregnant women attract me." He winked.

I had almost forgotten what it was like to get hit on. Geovane was of medium height, with black eyes and neatly trimmed short hair.

"Excuse me." I lifted my eyes to see Verena approaching. "You better leave before you end up six feet under..."

The woman smiled as if to expel him from the area.

"Yes, ma'am." Geovane stood up, nodding his head in respect to Verena, and quickly left.

"I thought that's what you wanted." I looked at the woman beside me, confused.

"Yes, and it worked. Santino allowed Geovane to come here, but men from the clan should never step into this area. Now it's up to San to keep an eye on Matteo so he doesn't take out poor Geovane." Verena sat down on the lounger next to me.

"Oh, heavens," I murmured, alarmed.

"Our plan worked." Verena clapped her hands, excited.

I heard my friend saying goodbye to her husband as she approached us, smiling with a wet body. Verena handed her the towel that was beside her.

"I'm sorry, but I couldn't keep the plan a secret. I ended up revealing everything to Valentino." Yulia looked angry with herself. "That... that... with all due respect, mother-in-law, but your son persuaded me. What a big jerk."

"I don't even want to know how that persuasion went." Verena motioned for Yulia to sit next to her.

My friend wrapped herself in the towel and sat down.

"Valentino promised he wouldn't say anything, although he scolded me for this behavior. Knowing Matteo as he does, Geovane is now in danger." Yulia rubbed her belly, panting as the twins kicked.

"Should I be worried?" I asked, anxious.

"No, because we have a clear law in the Cosa Nostra: do not attempt to take the life of any clan member. And theoretically, either Matteo admits what he feels for you, or he keeps quiet and goes on with his peaceful life," Verena said confidently. "Geovane didn't break any clan laws, so you can relax."

"That's reassuring," I murmured, sliding my fingers over my belly.

"Valentino said Matteo asked him if there was a chance the baby was his." My friend shared gossip I loved.

"And what did your husband say?" I asked, curious.

"He neither confirmed nor denied, just planted the seed of doubt in his mind. What are the chances of the consigliere going crazy?" Yulia smiled devilishly, just as I did.

"Or taking a turn in his life, right?" Verena added.

"Whether he takes a turn or not, I saw with my own eyes the man transform, wanting to go after poor Geovane." My friend was excited.

"Not poor, he was quite enthusiastic hitting on me. I'm amazed at how he came on so shamelessly, not caring about anything. Maybe I could even get back at him," I declared, mocking and laughing loudly.

"Then we'd really have a crazy consigliere." Verena began to laugh along.

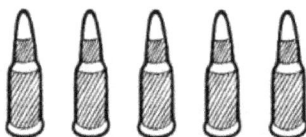

I SPENT THE ENTIRE afternoon by the pool with Yulia and Verena. I took a long shower, slowly applying my cream, loving the way it caressed my belly while my daughter responded with little kicks.

A knock on the door made me turn my face. Just to answer it, I grabbed the robe from the bed, tying it so that it covered my entire body.

I walked toward the door, opening it slightly, expecting it to be Verena or Yulia, but who I saw standing there was someone I never would have imagined.

"What do you want? You must have the wrong room," I said, sticking only my head out, revealing very little of my body.

"We need to talk." His voice directed at me made my whole body go on high alert, needing to be strong, needing to restrain myself from giving in.

"We have nothing to talk about." I started to pull my head back, about to close the door, but Matteo stopped me by holding it open.

"Yes, we do, and you know it!" His harsh tone made me exhale heavily.

"No, I don't know. All I know is that I hate looking at your face." I pushed the door with more force this time.

He was taken aback. He might have thought that I would let him in, that we would talk, and he would hear what he so desperately wanted: *that the child wasn't his*. I knew that's what Matteo wanted, but the beautiful little girl I was carrying inside me *was his*.

I leaned against the door, turning the key in the lock so he couldn't get in without my permission.

"You're pregnant, and if this child is mine, you'll bitterly regret hiding this pregnancy." From the other side of the door, I could hear his complaint.

"Did you forget that you called me vulgar? If you have a short memory, know that *I don't*," I declared, knowing he was still there listening to me.

"Nothing justifies hiding a pregnancy," he continued, trying to force a confession from me.

"Understand what you want," I let my voice sound with as much conviction as I could.

"We're talking about a child, *damn it*! It's not merchandise. You need to know that everything I carry is tainted, and if this child is mine, he will have the genes of a cruel, tormented man," Matteo kept on.

Without thinking, I just placed my hand on my belly, wanting to protect my little one from that man, trying to make Matteo back off even though I desired his touch.

"Live your solitary, boring, and dull life. My daughter will never be yours," I said firmly, with tears streaming down my face.

The way I spoke didn't reveal whether he was the father or not, just made it clear that Felicity would never be his. My little one would have all the love in the world, even if it meant keeping all the evil that surrounded us at bay.

Matteo might be charming, handsome, and flirtatious, but he had ruined me, said horrible things about me, hurt me in ways that made me determined to be strong for our daughter.

CHAPTER TWENTY

Billie

It took me a while to muster the courage to leave the room; perhaps it was my hunger that made me decide to go out.

I slowly went down the stairs, my hand gripping the railing, my eyes heading towards the living room, where I entered cautiously.

"Are you okay, dear?" Yulia asked as soon as she saw me.

"Yes, I'm fine. I just lay down on the bed and fell asleep for a bit," I replied with a half-smile.

"Being by the pool is wonderfully exhausting," my friend responded with a smile.

"Yes, can I go to the kitchen to see if there's something to eat?" I asked, knowing that it was late and they had probably already had dinner.

"We left a plate of food for you in the kitchen. Feel free to help yourself," Mrs. Verena winked at me.

I didn't quite understand what that meant, but I nodded and headed to the kitchen alone. I entered the quiet room, seeing a covered plate of food on the stone island. I went to it, sat on the stool, removed the cover, and noticed they had even left utensils there.

The smell reached my nose, and I closed my eyes, savoring the wonderful aroma.

I took the first bite, then the second, getting lost in the delicious plate of food. I might have been hungrier than I expected.

"Hello." I turned my face with my hand on my chest.

"Geovane," I said, widening my eyes.

"Sorry, did I startle you?" He leaned against the island next to me, a casual smile on his lips.

"Look, I was engaged in the arduous task of eating this delicious meal," I teased, noticing the first buttons of his shirt open, revealing a tattoo.

"You look even more beautiful with a slight blush." He lifted his hand and brushed it against my cheek.

I could easily give in to him, just to relieve that sexual frustration inside me. But it would only be sex; Geovane wasn't the type of man who made butterflies flutter in my stomach, nor did he evoke that floating-leg sensation.

"Nonsense." I turned my face forward, not blushing, still recovering from the shock.

"How long do you plan to stay here?" His hand held my chin, making me look at him again.

"I don't have a set time to return." I shrugged nonchalantly.

"We could go out sometime. There are many places we can't go to here out of respect for the Vacchiano family." Geovane didn't take his eyes off me, looking for an answer, and at that moment, I didn't even know what to say.

"Oh, go out? Sure, that could be nice," I said, clearing my throat several times. Was this part of the plan? Going out with another man?

"Okay, we'll arrange a place tomorrow." Winking, he turned and left me alone.

I turned my gaze back to the plate of food, twisting my mouth. What was that? Did I just accept an invitation to go out with a man?

I thought the plan was getting out of control, but surprisingly, it made me feel more alive, as if the pregnancy didn't nullify me at all. I was still sexy, beautiful, and full of life.

"You're not going anywhere with our *caporegime*!" That deep tone echoing in the room, that voice, yes, it made me shiver, lifted me off the ground, making the butterflies flutter in my stomach.

"Sorry?" I pretended not to understand what he had said, turning my face and being caught off guard by Matteo.

His hair was loose, seeming even damp, his beard perfectly outlining his features, with the first buttons of his shirt undone. I felt a bit tipsy from his chest, which I had once touched.

"I don't think I need to repeat myself; you're not going anywhere with our *caporegime*!"

"Oh, you mean *Geo*," I used a nickname for him, hoping to make Matteo think we were closer than he thought.

Matteo must have overheard the conversation behind the door to know that I was going out with Geovane. If he wanted to test him, he would do it in the best way he knew, by provoking him.

"Fuck how you call him; you're not going anywhere with him," his voice came out between clenched teeth, almost like a growl.

"And who's going to stop me? You?" I furrowed my brows, standing up from the stool while crossing my arms.

"Geovane isn't the right man for you; he treats all women like they're just a product..."

"Maybe I want to be just a product, or have you forgotten that you did exactly the same thing five months ago? You must be identifying with him; there's just one thing that separates you... he isn't as much of an asshole as you are," I threw it in his face, wanting him to feel the pain he made me feel.

"Don't compare me to another man," he growled, taking a step toward me.

"Too late, I already did." I shrugged. Even though I was terrified inside, I kept my head high, trying to appear indifferent.

"What are you doing here? Are you trying to test me, make me think this baby is mine?" Running his hand through his hair, he stopped moving and stood in front of me, too close, close enough for me to smell his masculine scent.

"The world doesn't revolve around you; I have a friend here, and whenever *I* want, I'm invited to come. I don't want to test anyone, especially since it's proven that you're a big arrogant who thinks he owns everything, but you're mistaken about that. Is this all because of a casual hookup? *Oh*, Italian, you need much more than that to get my attention." I turned my back, wanting to leave him talking to himself.

His fingers encircling my wrist pulled me closer, and as I was pulled, I turned, needing to grip his buttoned shirt to keep from falling. I looked up at him.

"We're having a conversation; don't turn your back on me," he growled through clenched teeth.

"We have nothing more to talk about; let me go before I scream," I shouted, trying to pull my hand free.

His eyes were half-closed, the desire to be thrown into those strong arms while he yelled at me, my mind resisting to keep me sober.

"You're not going out with Geovane!!!" he exclaimed in a terrifying whisper.

"I'll go wherever I want; don't treat me like I'm yours when I'm nothing." I pulled my arm with enough force to escape him.

"Billie Harris, you will regret every word you've said." I turned to him as I stopped in front of the kitchen door, knowing that I was at a safe distance to run if necessary.

"I hope you regret the ones you said to me as well, because if anyone is wrong here, it's not me," I responded, my eyes challenging his.

I don't know why, but whenever it came to Matteo, it was like my body went into alert mode, and all I wanted to do was provoke him.

Turning, I left quickly, breathless, needing to be alone in my room.

CHAPTER TWENTY-ONE

Billie

"Are you going out with him, friend?" Yulia asked that morning while we were having breakfast together.

"Getting into this game made me remember who I was before; I shut myself off, deprived myself of everything out of fear, fear that my pregnancy would be spread around as a mistake, the daughter of Hollywood's best couple in an unexpected pregnancy. I may not have planned to get pregnant, but my daughter will never be considered a mistake," I was honest with my friend about that.

"So, we're going to provoke the *consigliere* to the maximum level?" Yulia's black eyes sparkled.

"Full blast." I let out a small laugh. "Now that I've seen he really cares, I've seen the jealousy reflected in him, I'm going to make that mafioso eat the bread the devil threatened him with."

"I'm dying *to* see that result." The noise of people entering the breakfast room made us both go silent.

I raised my face, noticing that it was Valentino and his loyal sidekick, Matteo, who were coming through the door. The long-haired man immediately directed his gaze at me, glaring, seeming even a bit angry.

"Hello, darling." Yulia smiled at her husband as if they hadn't even slept together.

"I'm just here to let you know that we're heading out." Valentino stopped next to his wife, giving her a kiss on the top of her head.

"Oh, that's fine." My friend cleared her throat as if talking to her husband in a silent exchange of glances.

Matteo remained standing in front of the door, his eyes fixed on me, but I didn't do the same, feeling his gaze. He was probably still brooding over yesterday's events.

"Don't forget we have the appointment with the obstetrician today, so we can see our babies." Yulia ran her hand over her large belly, opening a big smile.

"I would never forget..."

"Alright, I know, I'm almost sure you forgot." My friend narrowed her eyes at her husband.

"Sorry, luckily I have you to remind me." He winked at his wife, straightening up and looking at me. "I hope you're enjoying your stay."

"Yes, loving it, it's been a while since I've felt this happy." I gave my best mocking smile.

"I guess all this happiness has a name..."

"And a surname too," I interrupted him, making it clear that the reason was Geovane. If it was about driving that long-haired man crazy, I'd do it the best way I knew how.

"Just be careful; Geovane isn't the type to get attached," Valentino continued trying to be as understanding as possible.

"That's alright, I don't want a father for my daughter; I just want a fling with ulterior motives," Yulia tried to contain her laughter and ended up choking on the food in her mouth.

By doing that, she drew our attention, and Valentino began patting his wife's back as if he were helping her.

"I'm fine," she said, recovering from her choking fit. "Sometimes I forget the friend I have."

Her gaze met mine, both of us sharing a knowing smile. We had always been great friends, sisters who found each other in college.

"You should be careful with your friends," Matteo's masculine tone, which had been silent until now, made its presence known.

"The one who should review the people around him is Valentino." I shrugged, not letting Matteo's words affect me, glaring at him.

"We should go before we need to break up a fight," Valentino said, turning as he left the dining room.

I was left alone with Yulia again, our eyes meeting, sharing a knowing look, and obviously, we were feeling the same thing.

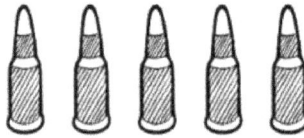

I LEFT MY FRIEND'S house, searching for the place where the mafia men were, wondering why they all had that serious look. As I got closer, I noticed the presence of the twins and Matteo. I wasn't looking for any of them, but for Geovane.

My footsteps were noticed by the men smoking cigarettes, leaning against the parked cars.

"Do you need something, Billie?" Valentino flicked the cigarette butt, handing it to Matteo to hold.

"Yes, I'm looking for Geovane," I asked about the man who had invited me out, wanting to know if our meeting was still on.

"He had to travel. They need temporary staff at our club in Las Vegas, and Geovane was the most effective *Caporegime*," Valentino said, assuming I would believe his words.

"Really?" My tone was questioning as my eyes locked on Matteo. "Is this your best strategy to keep that man away from me? It's pretty arrogant of you."

Matteo didn't say a word. He brought the cigarette to his mouth, ignoring me as if I were invisible.

"Asshole!" I stomped my foot, turning and leaving with heavy steps. At that moment, I wanted to punch Matteo's perfect face, make him swallow all his arrogance.

I entered the house and headed to the living room, where I found Mrs. Verena and Yulia sitting and talking about something. They stopped as soon as they saw me.

"You won't believe it." I crossed my arms, sitting on the couch.

"We just found out. Geovane was reassigned to Las Vegas; my husband just came by and told us," Verena said with a weak smile. "It all coincided with Geovane asking to go to Las Vegas a few days ago, and clearly, they took advantage of the opportunity to keep him away from you."

"So, it really is that Italian mafioso behind this?" I asked, still irritated.

"Yes, Matteo made the request. He's marking his territory, intimidating all the men in the clan so that none of them gets close to you," Verena seemed to know everything that was happening around.

"That big jerk, I want to punch that face. What does he think he is, making decisions about me? How can he think he can control me?"

"Well, that means we're doing our job right," Yulia tried to find a positive point.

"And it means I'm even more determined to provoke that arrogant long-haired man," I bit the corner of my lip, starting to come up with a new strategy.

"I love those sparkling eyes." My friend gave me a sly look.

"Even though I'm pregnant, he apparently doesn't care about the baby inside me, as if it doesn't affect him at all," I murmured, plotting something.

"In my view, Matteo is set on winning you back, or he just wants to keep all the men away from you. We can put that to the test," Verena joined in on my plan.

"We know it's no use using men now that he's declared that no one can get close to you. No one will go against Matteo's orders," Yulia declared.

"Well, I want him to swallow every word he said to me that day. I want to drive the mafioso crazy, but I can't forget that I have his child inside me. I can't let this backfire on me," I murmured, becoming anxious when it came to Felicity.

"I have an idea." Verena caught our attention, and I turned my eyes to her.

CHAPTER TWENTY-TWO

Matteo

Jealousy took over, and I practically demanded that Geovane be sent away before he acted out of turn and did something worse to one of our men, all because of damn jealousy.

Billie wasn't even mine, but it felt like she was, damn it! Just seeing him touch her chin made me break into a cold sweat. I wanted to blow Geovane's brains out. It was as if everything was spiraling out of control, with me no longer acting on my own behalf. The monster inside me was taking over.

No one was going to lay a finger on Billie Harris, not while she was under my watch!

I turned my face, seeing Valentino with that look of: *I told you so.*

He and Santino had warned me this would happen, that when she found out, she would be even angrier with me, but damn it, Billie was still here and without Geovane hovering around her all the time.

"You know what I really don't understand?" Santino declared, taking a drag from his cigarette, making a dramatic pause.

"Spit it out, Santino," Valentino grumbled at his brother.

"Why don't you go after her? Why treat her this way?"

"Every time I tried to talk to Billie, she came at me with all guns blazing. That's the reason." I shrugged my shoulders.

"And let's be honest, with good reason, right? You called her vulgar, and I bet you never apologized," Valentino continued defending his wife's friend.

"I didn't mean to say that. Billie will never be vulgar. I just spoke that way because I wanted her away from me."

"Strange way to handle your problems," Santino grumbled, rolling his eyes.

"What do you want me to do? I already ruined Juliana's life for years when I tricked her with a wedding that was never going to happen. I don't want to get attached to another woman and have to crush all her dreams," I declared, sighing, raising my hand to bring the cigarette to my mouth.

"In my opinion, you didn't love Juliana. At most, you liked having her around, a regular fuck, having a woman there with you. When I found out there was another man marrying my wife, I wanted to kill everyone in front of me. Cinzia was mine, always was mine, and the idea of another man touching what's mine drives me crazy," Santino wanted me to reflect.

None of that crossed my mind when Juliana married someone else. It was more about a petty jealousy watching her move on so quickly. What terrified me was the voracious presence of that blonde, how she devastated all my thoughts, her restless impulses. Always smiling, joyful, and often exuberant. Billie was exactly what Santino described.

Damn it! I went crazy seeing her being touched by another. But I couldn't admit that. I couldn't let anyone realize that I was becoming obsessed with Billie.

"He's stubborn, prefers to lose the woman rather than admit he might be feeling something real for her," Valentino's voice had that mocking tone.

"Go to hell," I grumbled.

"And if her child were yours, what would you do?" Santino drew my attention to him.

"I've thought about that scenario, and I admit that for a short time I wanted it to be true. That way, Billie would be forced to live with me, and I wouldn't have to ask her to stay."

"I've considered many possibilities about you, my friend, but never thought you were such a coward," Valentino retorted, reprimanding me.

"I don't want to become a sick man like my father. Having certain habits like his is enough to make me want to stay away from a relationship," I ran my hand through my hair, pushing it back.

"Brother, don't cling to that. I'm sure you won't be like your father," Santino declared, raising his hand and squeezing my shoulder.

Fortunately, the conversation took a different turn. I hated when the topic turned to my father.

I WASN'T USED TO BEING in the Vacchiano family's inner circle; I mostly stayed on the outside, my business was directly with the men of the family, although I had a great deal of respect for the women in the family.

From time to time, they'd invite me for dinner at the headquarters, but I usually declined. It wasn't that I didn't like them; living their reality was strange, nothing compared to what I had. A sadistic father and a masochistic mother, their madness went so far that he ended up taking her life.

As if living a perpetual punishment, my father never remarried and I didn't even see him with other women. He was still one of the *Caporegimes* of the Cosa Nostra, but he didn't work directly at the headquarters. Sometimes he would come to resolve some issues and then return to his home, accompanied by his men.

I lit my cigarette, walking through the darkness behind the headquarters, waiting for Valentino to finish his dinner. I wasn't hungry; I was just there so that when the Don was done, he would come to the hideout since we had more matters to discuss.

Before I even brought the cigarette to my mouth, I heard a sniffle, as if someone was crying. I followed the sound towards the cry, seeing her sitting on the stones that separated the headquarters from the sea that stretched out there.

I would recognize those blonde locks anywhere. Even with only the moonlight illuminating her, it was clear— it was Billie, and she was crying.

Without thinking, driven purely by impulse, I approached her. The woman, upon seeing me, started to get up, her eyes meeting mine.

"What are you doing here? Can't I even have a moment of privacy?" she quickly became rude.

"Did something happen?" I asked, not caring that she was trying to push me away.

"None of your business." She wiped under her eyes, cleaning away the tears.

"Billie?" I called her name as she walked past me. Her arm brushed against mine, making me turn and grab her elbow.

She was short, which made me lower my face.

"What do you want, huh? To insult me? To reduce me to nothing? What do you want from me, Matteo? Can't you see I want distance from you? Since you came into my life, you've only left me confused and angry," she spat out the words as if trying to rid herself of all the hurt, the hurt I caused.

"I... I..." nothing came out of my mouth, as if a furball had lodged itself inside me and I was frozen. I wanted to ask her not to feel this way, that nothing I had said was true, but I lost the chance when Billie forcefully pulled her arm away and headed towards the headquarters.

But I wasn't giving up; I practically ran after her.

CHAPTER TWENTY-THREE

Billie

All I wanted was to be alone, but it seemed that even that was impossible. Why did that arrogant mafioso keep finding me everywhere? What was his problem?

My hurried steps led me towards the house; it didn't seem so far when I came here.

With fingers wrapped around my wrist, my body was yanked backward by the force, causing me to stop walking.

"What the hell!" I growled, turning to face the tall man who looked at me, confused. Even with the place shrouded in darkness, the moonlight illuminated our faces.

"We need to talk." Matteo lowered his gaze towards me.

"We need to? No, we don't," I said, trying to pull my arm away in vain.

"Can you stop?"

"No, I can't. I don't want to talk to you, not now, not at this moment," I declared, taking a deep breath. I had just ended a call with my mother. After months without hearing from her, any news from her was rarely a good thing.

"What's wrong?" He genuinely seemed concerned.

"Nothing that concerns you." It wasn't like I could vent to Matteo, the man who had said the most horrible things to me.

"Billie, I can be a good listener." His touch softened on my hand.

"The thing is, it's too late for you to start giving me attention now," I resisted, not willing to give in.

"I'm sorry for what I said about you." Matteo took a step towards me, and without letting go of my wrist with his other hand, he caressed my skin, sliding his finger along my arm, making a tingling sensation spread through me.

"Don't apologize if what you're saying isn't true." I bit my lip, looking at the distant sea.

"It's true. I wouldn't say it if it weren't." His body stopped very close to mine, too close.

"Even so," I declared, trying to stay strong, not looking at him, remaining resistant.

"Have they told you that you're a stubborn *ragazza*?" Releasing my wrist, his fingers pressed against my chin, forcing me to lift my eyes and look at him.

"I don't care." I shrugged subtly.

Incredibly, that confrontation with Matteo was pushing my problems out of my mind. If there was one thing that mafioso was capable of, it was definitely pulling me out of all my comfort zones.

"Alright, alright." I crossed my arms since he wasn't holding them. "What do you want from me?"

I waited for him to speak. Matteo took a step back, making it easier for both of us to look at each other.

"I want to apologize for the way I spoke to you in Las Vegas," his voice sounded somewhat apprehensive.

"That's it?" I raised an eyebrow.

"Is there anything else I did wrong?" The mafioso, with an air of arrogance, twisted his lip as if trying to remember another factor.

"What about Geovane?"

"What about him?" Matteo gritted his teeth, tightening his jaw.

"Aren't you going to apologize for sending him away without any reason?"

"I have nothing to do with that..."

"Liar, you do, and I know it." I shook my head, making it clear that I didn't believe anything he said.

Matteo looked beyond me, his eyes lost in the sea. He knew that I knew everything, and he had clearly been caught red-handed.

"Geovane requested a transfer to Las Vegas, and now there's an opening."

"That makes it hard to believe your words." I rolled my eyes, making a move to turn away from Matteo.

"Alright, you win," he said through clenched teeth, grabbing my wrist again, forcing me to look at him once more. "Geovane requested the transfer, but I'm the one who made him leave now. I sent that man away before I broke one of my clan's rules and punched him in the face."

"And why would you do that?" I asked, clearly challenging him, wanting to see the mafioso admit in front of me that he was jealous.

"Because I set my eyes on you first. Even if not directly, indirectly, you're mine!" he roared, bringing his face even closer to mine.

"I don't know if you realize it, but I'm not an object for you to mark as yours." I moved my face closer to his, making it clear that I wasn't intimidated by him.

"Fuck it. As long as you're here at the headquarters, I'll ruin anyone who dares to get close to you," he snarled.

"Is that a threat?" At that moment, our noses were almost touching.

"If that's how you're taking it, then that's how it is." Taking a step back, I let out a forced laugh, rolling my eyes again.

"This is ridiculous. Everything about this situation is extremely ridiculous," I declared, turning back to him. "What's your point with all this? Why are you treating me this way? It was just a hookup, just a hookup!"

"That's what it was to you?" Matteo frowned in an amusing way.

"Yes, a good hookup, and nothing more." I shrugged my shoulders slightly, trying to seem indifferent, even though I was enjoying the whole game.

"That's not how it looks." His eyes traveled down my body, and the way he stopped at my belly made me a bit worried. "Who's the father of this baby?"

He asked again, leaving me confused, feeling guilty for maintaining the lie.

"It's not you," my voice faltered.

"You haven't answered my question. Who's the father of the baby?" he asked, growing more serious.

"It's not you. After all, we used a condom, as you said," I gasped, unable to control myself.

"Then why won't you answer my question? Who's the father of the baby?" It was like he was putting me against the wall, my legs going weak, fear overtaking my whole body.

I couldn't keep lying in the face of all that. I couldn't lie about a man's name; it felt like lying to my daughter too.

Matteo let out a long sigh, turning towards the sea, running his hand through his long hair, which, when loose, fell a little below his shoulder. It was incredible how that man seemed more and more handsome.

"Matteo," I said his name as if calling him, but deep down, I was saying the name of my daughter's father.

"Are you going to say his name now?" Matteo asked, turning back to me.

"His name is Matteo." I bit the corner of my lip as I revealed the whole truth, knowing that it could change everything between us.

CHAPTER TWENTY-FOUR

Matteo

His name is Matteo...

I kept repeating that a thousand times as I struggled to grasp what Billie had really said. *I'm the father?* Is there a child of mine in that small, rounded belly? *My child?* Or rather, a daughter? Since I had heard her referring to it as a girl.

I pressed her because I wanted that answer, and now that I had it, I didn't know how to handle the mix of emotions, as if a hole had opened beneath my feet and I was falling freely. My eyes were fixed on the small woman in front of me, waiting for some response from me. Everything I had sworn would never happen to me was now falling into my arms. *A daughter...*

I had to blink a few times, slowly, forcing myself not to panic, needing to keep my sanity.

"Just... just..." was all that came out of my mouth as I turned away.

I headed towards the sea, the huge rocks that separated the end of the property from the beach, my feet touching them, supporting my hand on them, jumping over the higher ones, the many times I had passed by them as a teenager with the twins making it easy to navigate.

I jumped over the last rock and landed in the sand, my shoes sinking into the loose sand. I placed one foot over the other, took off my shoes, bent down to remove my socks, leaving them in the corner.

I just needed to be alone, my torments thrown right in my face, like cursed stabs, my wounds I had thought were healed for years reopening, it felt as if I could feel my heart bleeding, tightening so loudly.

Hell! This couldn't have happened.

How did I allow myself to falter? I knew the monster that lived within me; I wasn't like Valentino or Santino. I carried the dirty blood of the De Lucas, all the men in that family had been monsters at some point in their lives.

I couldn't allow myself to do the same to Billie. I wasn't worthy of that child growing inside her.

I didn't stop walking; I knew where I was heading, knew where I wanted to go. It was as if all my demons forced me to see with my own eyes the man who made me witness the worst thing in a boy's life. Not all the lives I had taken compared to watching my mother's life slip away right in front of me.

My steps were confused, my mind dazed, time seemed to stand still. But there it was, the house of my childhood. The same one that was the cause of my worst nightmares.

I was a man; I shouldn't let those torments sway me. But at that moment, I felt like a kid, the same kid who had seen the shot fired in that room with the light on, reliving the scene in my mind.

Without stopping, I went towards the back entrance of the house. I needed to see it with my own eyes. I needed to torment myself a little more, facing the reason for all my demons.

My father didn't live in the same complex as the headquarters, but the beach connected the residences.

I stopped in front of the back door, where there was a window, the same one where my eyes had spotted my father, my older version. Even though I kept my hair long to not look like him, the genetics were there, screaming how alike we were, inside and out.

Carlo rose from his imposing armchair. Nothing had changed; he had gone on with his life, only changing the carpet where Mom had spilled her blood.

It didn't take long before I heard the sound of the lock, which was soon turned, and the door opened. As my eyes met my father's, he obviously frowned at my state, my hands clenched into fists since I had left the headquarters, my jaw clenched to the point of pain.

"Matteo, what are you doing here? Why are you like this? What happened?" Carlo asked, opening the way for me to enter his house.

There had never been a fight between us; only the distance made it clear that we weren't compatible.

"Why? Why?" I asked as I entered the room, my eyes focusing on the clean carpet. It was no longer the same; I got lost in the vision of that space, the many times my mother had been loving towards me, her comforting hugs, the lingering kisses on my cheek.

"What are you talking about?" He walked past me, holding a cane.

"Why are we like this? Why did you kill my mother?" I turned my eyes, following his movements until I saw him sit in his armchair. Obviously, we had never talked about this before.

"Why do you want to know about this now?" He set the cane down beside him.

"For years I lived with this image, carrying within me the need to avoid any woman to not hurt her. Marriage is a torment when I think I want to marry. It was easy to send Juliana away; I thought I wanted her by my side, but when she married someone else, it was easier than I thought to forget her. But now..." I stopped speaking, closing my eyes, squeezing them tightly as all I could think about was Billie.

"Now there's another woman." I nodded my head in confirmation.

"She is different, *she is... she is...* perfect, in all the wrong ways, perfect, and I can't, it's as if there's a wall stopping me from going to her." I opened my eyes, focusing them on my father.

"If she's all that." Carlo let out a long sigh, his eyes seeming to lose themselves in something distant. "Stay away from her. Don't make the same mistake I made. I killed the love of my life, and I'll never forgive myself for it. Living this shitty life is my punishment for taking your mother's life. The monster that lives in me lives in you. If this woman is your downfall, if this woman has you, if you want what's best for her, send her away. Before you make the biggest mistake of your life."

His words cut into my ears like sharp knives. It felt like I was in walls closing in around me. *No, no, no, no...*

I wouldn't forgive myself if another man touched what was mine, but I also would never forgive myself if I were the one to do any harm to her.

CHAPTER TWENTY-FIVE

Billie

Alone there, staring into nothing, I wondered where Matteo had gone, why he had left like that. So many questions, but no answers.

In my mind, I had created a million theories about how he would react, but none of them were like this. Without a word from him, without knowing what he thought about our daughter, he just left and left me there alone.

I ran my hand over my arms, feeling the sea breeze, a slight shiver running through my body. I turned and went back to the house. Should I tell Yulia about all this madness?

I had even forgotten about my mother's phone call; that worry seemed minimal compared to the reaction of my daughter's father.

Mom had told me not to return to New York, as she and Dad were about to close the biggest success of their lives, and nothing could negatively influence it, not even my pregnancy without paternity.

I wanted to be alone; that was how Matteo found me. I wanted to be with my daughter, to make her understand that I would never do that to her, even though she was still in my womb.

I entered my friend's house; it was always so full of people. I never saw myself alone there; it was like a huge family that never left her alone. I know Yulia spent most of her childhood alone, and she loved it all, that enormous family support.

I wiped my eyes to make sure there were no more traces of tears. I saw my friend's husband next to her, so I would just let him know that the mafioso had gone somewhere I didn't know.

"Valentino," I said in a low tone, stopping beside him as he was at the end of the couch with his arms around his wife's shoulders.

"Yes?" He lifted his face, looking at me with curiosity.

"It's about Matteo." Anxious, I cleared my throat, unsure how to speak. "Well, *I...* told him. I ended up being pressured, and I said it. Maybe it wasn't exactly the right way, maybe he just wanted me to say the baby wasn't his. Anyway, I said, Matteo knows my daughter is his... *and... and...* his reaction was strange..."

"Where is he?" Valentino asked, getting up from the couch.

"He... he..." I stammered, "went towards the sand, and I lost sight of him. I don't know where he went."

"I know where he went, to the worst place he could go." Valentino ran his hand through his hair, as if scratching his head with such force that it showed.

Turning to Yulia, he bent down and kissed her forehead, saying he would be stepping out.

I sat next to my friend as her husband left without even telling me where he was going or mentioning what Matteo had done.

"I think I made the wrong choice, friend," I murmured with a heavy sigh.

"Billie, it's not your fault. Matteo is a man full of torment." She gave a forced smile, the kind I recognized well, when she wanted to comfort someone.

"Can we go upstairs and be alone? Just the two of us like we were in college?" I asked, and Yulia nodded.

We got up from the couch silently and went to the room where I used to sleep.

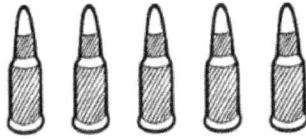

I PRETENDED TO BE ASLEEP when I heard the whispers next to my bed. After hours of talking with my friend Yulia, I had fallen asleep, but it wasn't a deep sleep; there was no way I could simply sleep soundly after the recent events.

"Did you find him?" Yulia whispered, as if speaking to someone.

"Yes, he was at his father's house," I recognized Valentino's voice.

"How is he?" They spoke so softly that it took effort to try to hear them.

"It's Matteo, so you can be sure it will be complicated for him to accept, after everything he's been through, having to break his own life convictions. I really don't know how he'll accept this," Valentino's words made me tremble inside, tremble in a negative way.

What could be wrong with Matteo, after all? Why was no one talking to me about this?

The bed beside me shifted, making me realize that Yulia had gotten up.

"If Matteo does anything to my friend, he will make an enemy for life, and I'm not talking about Billie, I'm talking about myself. I'll break his face," Yulia's words were so much like her, I had no doubt about her words, after all, we always protected each other.

I heard her husband's soft laugh, and their footsteps indicated that they were leaving the room, soon everything became completely silent. I was alone there.

Maybe I always felt partly alone, and this was just another time. But I felt that things would change, running my hand over my belly, smoothing my little bump, I felt her tiny kick, knowing that I would never be alone again, after all, I had her.

ONCE AGAIN, I WENT down for breakfast, and he was nowhere to be seen, not a trace of my daughter's father. It had been five days since he had learned about Felicity and simply disappeared from the house.

Yulia told me that he only went outside the house, just to talk to some mafia men, he didn't enter, he didn't linger in his visits, it must have been just a short period of time, so short that I never saw him.

Sitting there in the chair, I looked at the lavish breakfast table.

I was getting unaccustomed to it, always with a full table and many people, lots of laughter and conversations, everything I had never experienced before, it even felt like a dream if it weren't for that small obstacle, Matteo.

I felt some pitying looks in my direction, but it was as if everyone respected me enough not to mention Matteo's name.

That morning, I decided to do something different. He didn't want to accept that we had a child? Fine, but I wouldn't accept him stopping coming to that house, changing his life, making those people look at me with pity.

"Valentino?" I called my friend's husband who was sitting at one end of the table while his father was at the other end.

"Yes?" His eyes fixed on mine.

"I want to know where Matteo's house is. I'm going to have a talk with him. He may not accept our daughter, but I won't accept him stopping his life and coming to this house, making people look at me with pity," I said, looking at everyone there. I knew Mrs. Verena wanted to argue, but Valentino spoke first.

"I believe your decision is the best. I'll have one of our men at your disposal to take you to his house, but I won't inform Matteo. Otherwise, he will leave the house."

I just nodded in agreement, my hands clenched together, feeling the anger starting to grow inside me. Matteo could do anything, but he wouldn't give me the silent treatment.

All Felicity needed was me; that man could go on with his life, just forgetting that I existed.

CHAPTER TWENTY-SIX

Matteo

I crossed my leg, reading Valentino's message, which said he didn't need my help that morning. That kind of message had become necessary; I didn't want to run into Billie for now.

It might be selfish of me, but she was much better off without me. *They were.*

It wasn't good; nothing about me could do her any good. It was better that Billie moved on with her life without my presence.

My decision was already made; it would be better this way. I wouldn't bring any shame to Billie; I wouldn't be the father tormenting my daughter's life...

Daughter, every time that word came to my mind, I felt my heart tighten, contracting at the sensation of feeling her slipping through my fingers. As if I was losing her.

But I decided to follow my father's decision; his advice was based on someone who had lived through what I might face in the future. Valentino even tried to make me understand that I wouldn't do what my father did, that we were two different people. But my friend didn't understand, didn't understand that the blood of a killer ran through my veins.

I finished my breakfast, got up from the chair, knowing I wouldn't need to go out. I looked around and realized how boring my life could be. Alone...

The doorbell rang, making me turn my face. I furrowed my brows, not remembering inviting anyone over. The doorbell rang again, this time repeatedly, as if the person was pressing it over and over.

Damn! I turned the key and opened the door, taking a step back in surprise, and saw the person I least expected standing there. Billie.

"Finally," without being invited in, she breezed past me like a small whirlwind.

I turned my body as I followed her steps and pushed the door to close it. Billie stopped in the middle of my living room, looking around before turning her angry eyes in my direction. It was clear she was mad.

"We need to talk," she said.

"Need to?" I put my hand in my pants pocket.

"Of course!" She crossed her arms, drawing my attention to them resting over her belly, that small bump.

"Alright, then start." I raised an eyebrow, waiting for her to speak, after all, it was her who took that action.

"How can you be like this? So indifferent, I told you something and you were cold, distancing yourself, making everyone feel sorry for me." Billie dropped her arms to her sides, slapping them.

"Sorry for you?" I frowned, puzzled.

"Yes, because now I'm not just a pregnant woman, I'm the pregnant woman who also had her child rejected." Billie's eyes widened, she almost ran at me and grabbed my neck.

I didn't respond immediately, thinking about what she had said. After all, we hadn't talked, but my attitude made it clear that I wanted nothing to do with her.

"Are you going to stay silent? Are you going to remain an insensitive man?" she asked, her eyes filled with tears, revealing that Billie was controlling herself from crying in front of me.

"I'm sorry, I don't know what to say..." My voice faltered as Billie picked up a decorative ornament from the coffee table.

The sound of that small crystal shattering on the floor showed how angry she was with me, and I took a step back.

"I DON'T WANT ANYTHING FROM YOU!" she shouted.

Now with tears streaming down her face, making me feel dirty, a damn arrogant for treating Billie this way, she certainly didn't deserve my indifference.

"And I don't doubt that," I declared, taking a step toward Billie.

"Then why are you doing this?" She moved even further away from me.

"I... I..." I cleared my throat, this didn't usually happen to me, I didn't clear my throat in situations that confused me. "I just can't be what you expect me to be."

"You don't even know what I want from you." She rolled her eyes.

"Then tell me," I asked, trying to understand her.

"I don't want you to change anything in your life, I don't want you to stop coming to Valentino's house because of me. Do you understand? It's been five months since we've been alone, we don't need you. You don't need to play the father of the year, I don't need anything from you. Just don't stop coming to the house, it makes everyone pity me when I can be everything my daughter needs." Hearing the truth thrown in my face hurt, hurt more than I ever thought it could.

A silence fell over the room, I clenched my hands in my pockets, the anger overtaking me, not because of her, but because of myself. I was being the monster.

"Can you just do that for me? It's not too much to ask, you can keep pretending I don't exist," she broke the silence, demanding a response from me. I needed to say something.

"Yes," I murmured, that was all that came out of my mouth.

My body was frozen, my feet felt glued to the floor. It was as if my heart was screaming not to let them go, but my mind in denial was telling me how much of a mistake it would be to accept that paternity, that woman. I wanted them, with all my strength, *I wanted*, but I couldn't... I couldn't...

"I think that's all, since it's impossible to have a conversation with you," she spoke again, turning around, her heels echoing in my living room.

Billie was leaving, the woman who came to my house wanting me to return to my routine so that no one would pity her. She wanted to move on, she would have that child and didn't need me.

"Billie," I called her name as I heard the sound of my door opening.

I don't know why I did it, but giving in to my heart, I went towards her, my legs recalling what it was like to walk, and I stood face to face with the mother of my child.

"What do you want, Matteo?" she asked, as if she was finally expecting an action from me.

"I want you, I want her..., *but..., but...,*" I closed my eyes, the confusion driving me crazy. "But I'm afraid, very afraid...

I was honest, I wasn't lying to her. My demons existed, and they were there to torment me, to make me always falter.

"Afraid of what?" she asked in a whisper.

"I'm a monster, nothing about me is good. I carry the blood of monsters within me...

"If you're not more specific, I won't understand. After all, when I think of a monster, it's a totally different appearance than yours that comes to mind." Her eyes scanning my body made it clear that Billie would never change her authentic way of dealing with life.

"Come on, I'll explain, and then you can tell me what you think," I asked her to follow me back to the living room.

"I don't need to worry, you won't turn into a werewolf or something like that?" Billie asked as she followed me.

I didn't answer her question, knowing she was nervous and, as a result, tended to talk too much.

CHAPTER TWENTY-SEVEN

Billie

I went back to the living room, choosing to sit on the sofa. Matteo did the same, sitting across from me with the coffee table between us.

"I'm going to say everything, and I want you to just remain silent," he requested. We hadn't spent much time together, but it felt as though we knew each other so well.

"Alright," I affirmed, nodding my head.

Matteo took a moment, drawing in a deep breath, making me increasingly anxious as he prepared to speak. I crossed my legs, shifting on the sofa until he finally began:

"When I was eleven years old, my father killed my mother, he killed her right in front of me. It wasn't him, it was like the monster inside him, in an impulsive act, without thinking clearly, he took my mother's life." Matteo looked at the floor as if reliving that moment. "My father regretted it, but the shot was fatal. I saw him kneeling, begging for her to come back, but my mother would never return. They didn't have a stable marriage, it was more like a sadomasochistic relationship. I often heard him hitting her, heard her crying, begging, pleading for him to stop, but deep down, she loved him, a passion I'll never understand. My mother had a surreal dependency. While he reduced her to nothing, she loved him more."

He stopped speaking, and I stayed quiet, clasping my fingers together. All I could think about was an eleven-year-old boy witnessing his mother's death, the cries, how that must have tormented him.

"Throughout my life, I swore I would never go through that. I swore up and down that I would never marry, that I would never bring a child into this world, all out of fear, knowing the damn genes I carry. I don't want a child to witness what I saw, I don't want to spend the rest of my life crying over something I did. I don't want to kill my wife, the woman I chose to marry. Living this is like reliving those years," he opened up, revealing what was inside him, his true torments.

I remained silent, waiting for him to say more, for the first time at a loss for words, not knowing how to proceed.

"This is the truth, this is me, a man half-formed." Matteo raised his eyes, fixing them on me. I blinked a few times, and when I finally began to speak:

"Are you living someone else's fear?"

"You would never understand," he wanted to seem misunderstood.

"I definitely don't understand you. I grew up in a facade family. My parents only used me for the media, wanting to show everyone how perfect we were. Behind the cameras, I was forgotten. My childhood and adolescence were spent at a boarding school. My first real friend was Yulia. To everyone, I had the perfect life and was rebellious for always having everything. But no, I didn't have the basics, what should be the simplest thing: the love of my parents. All I wanted was to spend Christmas with my family, celebrate my birthdays with both of them. Until five months ago, I believed their words, believed they wanted me so we could be a real family, *but no...* their priority was always their careers." I forced a smile. "Now they don't even want me around anymore, all because I got pregnant and apparently don't know who the father of my child is. Not that I need them. After all, I will be everything she needs, even if it means it's just me and her against the world."

I said everything. I had a broken past too, but that didn't mean I let my fears dominate my thoughts.

Matteo fell silent, unsure if he had heard what I just said. It was clear that while he was running scared from a future, I was moving forward as if I wanted to grab everything life offered me.

"I'm sorry for everything I said about you," Matteo's voice was low, but he spoke with conviction.

"You've already apologized," I said with a half-smile.

"Yes, but it wasn't quite right how we ended things." He didn't smile.

"You're forgiven. Well..." I stood up from the sofa, looking around, letting out a forced sigh. It was foolishness on my part to imagine living in that big house, seeing our daughter running on that floor. "We don't have anything more to talk about. I've accomplished what I came here for."

I bit the corner of my lip because I wanted him to start coming to the house again, to pretend nothing happened between us.

Matteo also stood up from the sofa, rubbing his hand on his pants, making his nervousness clear.

"I want you to come live in my house."

"What?" I interrupted him, turning my face quickly. That request came out of nowhere.

"That's what you heard. I want you to come live in my house. I want you here. I want to know what it's like to have you living here."

"No! Are you crazy? I'm not an experiment to come live here just so you can see what it's like to have me in your house. You must be out of your mind," I cut him off again, widening my eyes.

"I'm not talking about an experiment. I just want you here. I want you to tell me more about our daughter."

"No!" I insisted again, cutting him off. "Just minutes ago you wanted me away from you. You didn't even want to know about our daughter. You refused. I'm not going to accept this. I'm not going to come running to your house just because you asked."

"I thought that's what you wanted." Matteo ran his hand through his hair, pushing it back.

"I never said I wanted to live with you. I only talked about our daughter because I was pressured, but don't think I'm here begging for you to accept me," I was honest in my words.

"I really don't understand you..."

"Look, Italian, think about your new attitude changes. I'm not going to move in with you just for you to think I'm not good enough for your torments the next day. No, I'm no fool to run to your arms." I shook my head, placing my hand on my belly, noticing that his eyes followed my movement.

"You're right," he murmured anxiously, not taking his eyes off my belly. "I'll take you to the headquarters."

"You don't need to. I have a driver," I declared, wanting to escape his curious looks.

"I thought you wanted me to start coming to the headquarters, so I'll go with you," he said seriously, walking around the room to grab his things like his phone and wallet.

"I'm just afraid of these changes in your opinions." I frowned, being guided by him toward the door.

CHAPTER TWENTY-EIGHT

Billie

Surprisingly, Matteo accompanied me to the Vacchiano house. Our journey was in complete silence, as I was apprehensive about what we might discuss.

That day felt strange. In a short time, I went from being irritated and angry, wanting to strangle that mobster, to trying to understand his demons.

I know everyone handles their torment in their own way, but given all the adversities life has thrown at me, I can't wrap my head around the fact that Matteo simply prefers to abandon everything.

We entered the headquarters together. Perhaps our being together could be a sign of sealed peace, without those pitying looks directed at me. Following my steps, we entered the room.

Everyone was there, including Valentino's sister and his sister-in-law, with whom I was on good terms. However, there was a woman with long black hair whom I hadn't met yet.

"Matteo," she said, her eyes shining when she spotted the man behind me. I widened my eyes as I felt Matteo's hand tighten around my waist, as if we were intimate.

"Juliana," he said her name, and I remembered her—the same name that made him cry his eyes out when we had our brief encounter in Las Vegas.

"Oh..." the beautiful woman cleared her throat, looking at my belly. "So it's true?" The disappointment in her voice was evident.

Being caught in that crossfire wasn't exactly what I wanted. After all, this woman had always wanted something from Matteo, and at that moment, it was me she was dealing with.

"It's true that my child is his? Yes. It's true that we're together? No." I turned my face, glaring at the mobster. If he thought he could use me to make her jealous, he was sorely mistaken.

In response, I received a growl from the mobster.

"Ah, but you really don't know me, hairy Italian." His serious expression softened in response to my reprimand.

"It's good to know that I'm starting to be treated as I was before," he whispered just loud enough for me to hear.

I rolled my eyes and moved away from him, heading toward Yulia, where there was an empty seat, and I needed to sit down.

"Valentino is in the office, Matteo," my friend Yulia said, even though he hadn't asked, as if the man was surplus to the room.

"Thanks." Matteo turned and left.

I knew everyone was eager to hear about my conversation with him, but I wasn't sure if I should comment on anything, given that his ex-girlfriend—or ex-fiancée, I wasn't sure what she was—was present.

Everything became silent, as the assumption was that the two of us might end up arguing over that man. Something I certainly would not do.

"You don't need to be silent because of my presence," Juliana finally spoke up. "Seriously, it's all over. I'm married, I have a husband, and a little son on the way..." She touched her small belly. "Matteo is in the past, a distant and exhausted love, tired of waiting for him to make a move."

Her expression softened, it was clear she must have loved him deeply, but wanted something every woman dreams of—a family.

"Dear, you made the best choice," Verena began. "We all knew he would only lead you on."

But Juliana kept her eyes on me, still confused.

"You know what I don't understand? How did you manage to get pregnant? For God's sake, we were together for years and he was never careless. — She genuinely seemed curious. "Sorry, but deep down I'm jumping for joy. What I asked him for, he's now having with a woman he barely knows. Is there a greater punishment for that man?"

She wasn't speaking in an accusatory tone but rather as if she was surprised and somewhat radiant.

"I wouldn't define my pregnancy as a punishment." I twisted my lip in a gesture of discomfort. "But I don't know how I got pregnant, and neither does he. We were too drunk for either of us to remember anything."

I shrugged, trying in vain to recall our first meeting, where neither of us had any memories.

"Sorry for the way I expressed myself. I don't want you to think I still love him. I love my husband. I only held a small grudge against Matteo. It's not that I want anything with him, because I don't want anything anymore..."

"Ah, I have nothing with Matteo. It was just sex." I shrugged, being overly honest in my way of speaking.

"That makes me even happier. After all, I was too nice to that man. He deserves someone who treats him like just sex. If you want a tip, don't let him boss you around." Juliana seemed like a good woman.

"Don't worry." I gave a wry smile, feeling Yulia's hand touch mine.

The women started chatting among themselves, but Yulia wanted to know more about our conversation.

"Did everything go well?" she asked quietly so that only the two of us could hear.

I ended up telling her everything, from the table ornament I broke to his declaration where he opened up to me, revealing his torments, and even the crazy request to move in with him.

"So, are you going to move in with him?" my friend asked, knowing that even if I said no, deep down my answer could be different.

"Look, I admit the proposal affected me, but I can't be vulnerable, I can't just give in like that. He changed his mind too quickly; it could have been just a spur-of-the-moment thing. Although I was slightly tempted by that decision. No, I'm not going to accept, not like this, not without proof that he really has changed his mind." I shrugged my shoulders once more.

"You're right. I'd be happy if you two moved in together; I'd have my friend here with me all the time. But I understand that the mobster needs to work hard to earn your approval." Yulia winked conspiratorially.

"I don't know why, but I love making a man work for it." I returned my friend's smile, biting the corner of my lip.

Our conversation eventually merged with the other women's discussions, and the topic of Matteo was forgotten, which was great for me, as I couldn't get that crazy conversation out of my mind during my alone time.

After all, he wanted me to move in with him. Even if it was for our daughter, I had never been asked to move in with someone, and for that reason, I needed to stay guarded against certain feelings.

CHAPTER TWENTY-NINE

Matteo

"So, does this mean you won't be staying away from our headquarters anymore?" Valentino asked with a hint of mockery, propping his feet on the mahogany of his desk.

"No," I declared, knowing I'd have to endure their teasing now.

"What made you change your mind?" Santino, who was present, wanted to know.

"There's only one person who could make me change my mind." I shrugged, accepting the cigar Santino handed me.

"It's funny how when I told you not to give up, you were very adamant about your opinion, which still worries me." Valentino raised his eyebrows.

"I still don't know, it's all very new. One thing I'm sure of is that I couldn't stand seeing another man touching Billie. Even though I'm afraid to acknowledge whatever feelings are binding us, it's different—everything about that woman is different." I sighed, running my hands through my hair.

"You know you might be falling for her." Santino made me roll my eyes as I brought the cigar to my mouth, inhaling its essence.

"You don't need to drastically change your opinion; you could start by testing what it would be like to live with her. Have you thought about inviting her out? Maybe getting to know each other better?" I looked at Valentino, holding the cigar between my fingers.

"Maybe I went overboard asking her to move in with me." I forced a smile. "Obviously, Billie declined and even called me crazy."

"I'd be surprised if she had accepted," Don mocked. "Will you give up, or will you keep trying?"

"I want Billie. I want her in my house. I don't know how exactly I want her, but I know I want that woman under my roof," I was honest.

I might have changed my mind quickly, but one thing was clear: I wanted Billie under my roof, where I could keep track of all her movements, know who she was seeing and what time she was coming back.

"And what about your daughter?" Santino wanted to know.

"At first, I thought I could be a terrible father, maybe I still do, but it never crossed my mind to refuse the baby. I wanted her, even though I was scared. I wanted her, but from a distance. And if I cause any harm to them?" I brought the cigar to my lips, the sound of that shot my father fired at my mother echoing in my head. What if the roles were reversed, and it was Billie in her place?

"Matteo, you need to get that out of your head. You are, and will never be, like your father. Moreover, Mom once said your mother was completely submissive to your father, and that they had a completely abusive relationship, even mistreating her in front of others. I would doubt Billie would ever become submissive to you, and besides, if you were like him, you would never have had a healthy relationship with Juliana, not to mention how you kept stringing her along." Valentino flashed a big forced smile as he took the cigar I offered him.

I shook my head, my thoughts racing. The image of Juliana was there, near me, in the headquarters' lounge. And nothing happened; there was no frantic urge to rush to her, to hold her in my arms. Nothing—it was like seeing an old acquaintance.

But deep down, I wanted her to feel that I had moved on too, that even though she had thrown in my face that I'd die unhappy and alone, I wanted to prove it was all a lie. Although that was a mistake, since Billie would never agree to fake something just to affect another woman.

Talking about my parents made me angry and sad, so I changed the subject, returning to discussing the Cosa Nostra, advancing paperwork for a new associate who wanted to join our clan. This associate was a good deal, a supermarket chain owner who wanted our security services. By joining us, he would receive total protection in exchange for allowing our men to enter his territory to sell our illicit substances.

I DESCENDED THE STAIRS alongside Valentino. Santino had left, needing to handle matters with a *caporegime*.

In the room remained a few women, including Juliana. But my focus wasn't on her; it was on the little one who also belonged to me.

Billie was distracted, talking with Yulia, her lips adorned with a beautiful smile, making her eyes narrow when she grinned.

I approached them, my steps noticed by the two women closest to me. Billie looked into my eyes as if she already knew I wanted to speak with her.

"Can we step outside to talk? It'll be quick," I emphasized, knowing she might refuse.

With a long sigh, Billie agreed. She stood up, her dress clinging to her body was not vulgar but deliciously highlighted her figure.

I waited for her to go around the couch, and we headed to the back of the house.

"Are you and Yulia about the same stage of pregnancy?" I asked, curious, knowing that if she got pregnant when we were in Las Vegas, it was when Valentino was on his honeymoon.

"Yes, just a few days apart," she answered promptly. "Are you going to accept it just like that? Without a test, without anything, that the baby is yours? After all, you called me vulgar..."

"That was me trying to push you away, I should have never been that low," I grumbled as we left the headquarters and walked across the lawn.

"You certainly know how to insult a woman," she said beside me, stopping next to a tree and looking up at me.

"Billie, I just wanted some way to make up for my mistake," I said, lowering my eyes.

"No, it can't be fixed. It's not like you can go back in time and change it. That doesn't exist, it's not possible." She crossed her arms. "But as I've said before, you're forgiven, just can't forget how shitty you acted."

Silence filled the space between us. I let out a long sigh, knowing I needed to stick to my initial plan.

"I want you to know that I still want you in my house. I want you to live there with me. It doesn't have to be as a couple, I just want you in my home..."

"Why the hell would I live with you? To see you with other women?" She raised an eyebrow.

"We can set some rules if you think it's better," I continued to insist.

Billie remained silent, not responding.

"Come out for dinner with me tonight, and we can talk about it," I invited her.

"Are you asking me out on a date?" She frowned in a funny way.

"Yeah, you could say that. A date between two acquaintances, with no ulterior motives."

"Alright, a date might be nice." She flashed a big, genuine smile, one of those beautiful, radiant smiles. "It's better; this way, you can practice all your persuasion techniques."

"Is 8 PM good?" I asked.

"That's fine." She shrugged, and without giving me a chance to say more, she turned and walked away.

I stood there alone, watching her walk away. She seemed to have more curves, more ass, more tits—damn! I needed to stop savoring the image of Billie's perfect body.

CHAPTER THIRTY

Billie

I stopped in front of the mirror, analyzing my outfit. I chose a floral dress, not a striking color but a neutral shade.

A knock sounded at my door. I turned my body, my eyes meeting my friend, who immediately broke into a broad smile.

"You look beautiful." Yulia came closer to me. "He's downstairs..."

"Your husband is here, isn't he?" I pursed my lips.

"And my brother-in-law too..."

"Alright, I'll be ready for the jokes then." I rolled my eyes, knowing that mocking each other was something that family loved to do.

I grabbed my phone from the bed, my heels softly echoing on the floor as we left the room. Even though I was pregnant, wearing small heels didn't bother me.

I went down the stairs, one step at a time, my eyes falling on him at the bottom, the most handsome man I had ever seen. Matteo had his thick hair down to his shoulders, his brown eyes fixed on me. He had even shaved, not completely but trimmed, making the design of his beard more pronounced.

Before I could approach him, he came to meet me, extending his hand, the first buttons of his shirt open as usual.

"Let's go before the twins start with their jokes," I requested with a smile, trying to be discreet.

Matteo simply nodded, taking my hand. His was so large it covered mine completely. We managed to leave the headquarters without incident. A car was waiting for us, but what surprised me most was that the front door next to the driver was open for me. I sat down, turning my face and seeing Matteo sit beside me.

"So, you know how to drive?" I asked, half teasing.

"It would be embarrassing if I didn't." Matteo started the car, and through the rearview mirror, I could see two other cars following us. We were being escorted.

I didn't let the silence settle between us; I quickly started asking questions.

"How was today?" The way he raised his eyebrow made it clear he didn't understand my question. "How was it meeting Juliana?"

My curiosity got the better of me.

"More normal than I expected. I think she's just become a person, any person." He shrugged nonchalantly, not looking at me.

"And before, what was she?" I could admit that I was feeling a slight pang of jealousy at that moment.

"Let's just say she was *the one*, you know, the one your eyes search for first in a crowd, the one you always want by your side." His face turned, and his eyes met mine.

It was clear that Matteo had experienced what love was, while I didn't even know what love between a man and a woman felt like.

"I think I should know what it's like..."

"Wait, you've never been in love with anyone?" Matteo, who had been looking at the road, turned his gaze back to me.

"I was more of the girl who just wanted to party. I spent most of my years stuck in that boarding school, and when I finally got my freedom and started college, all I wanted was sex, drugs, and orgies," the way I spoke made Matteo narrow his eyes at me, which made me laugh out loud. "Come on! The best part of college is the parties, but I lied about the drugs; it was only alcohol. I was the queen of all the parties."

I leaned back in the car seat, running my hand over my belly.

"God forbid my daughter does half of what I did," I joked, with a touch of affection.

"I don't think I'm ready for that." Matteo's face was pale, as if he were genuinely worried.

He signaled and pulled the car over to the side of the road, turning to me abruptly.

"Orgies? You participated in orgies?" He looked like he was going to strangle me at that moment.

"Who hasn't? Well, Yulia hasn't; she always left before the best part of the party. But I stayed until the end, drank until the last drop of alcohol as if there were no tomorrow," I continued, frightening the mafioso.

"Tell me it's all a lie, that you're saying this to terrify me."

"It's all true; I have no reason to lie. Now that I have this little bump inside me, I can say I've changed, I've changed for her." I gave a small smile, looking at my belly.

"You criticized me for changing my mind suddenly, but it seems you've changed too." I looked up at him again.

"Five months is different from five hours. You haven't even completed a day yet." I raised an eyebrow.

"I've never acted on impulse in my life; I've always been the type to calculate everything, think of all the pros and cons. And now, I simply don't want to think, I don't want to know what tomorrow will bring. I don't want my torment to make me falter. All I want is to have you two in my home," he said with a surreal conviction in his voice.

"You know we're talking about a baby, a baby that demands time, that will cry during the nights, requiring our attention, and depending on how things go, I'll also need a support network, people who can be by my side when I feel weak." That last part terrified me the most, considering the only person I had was Yulia, and she was also pregnant. I couldn't count on her.

"I can be all of that, I can be your person," Matteo said, his finger lifting to touch my chin, caressing it gently. "Come live with me, Billie, let me take care of both of you."

At that moment, I wanted to beg him to grab me, sit me on his lap, his muscular legs, and kiss me, kiss me as if there were no tomorrow. *Damn pregnancy hormones.*

"Just hours ago, you didn't even know if you could take care of us, you were afraid of your torments..."

"We can try, we can come up with ways to make me realize if I'm losing control. I won't lie, I'm scared, but my fear isn't greater than my sudden desire to have you with me." I bit the corner of my lip.

The mafioso slowly moved closer to me, his inviting lips making me remember the delicious kisses he knew how to give.

"Be mine, Billie." I melted, my already weak legs seeming to turn to jelly, his husky tone hitting right at the core of my desire, making me completely wet for him.

"Damn it..." I murmured, closing my eyes and sighing heavily, feeling his lips brush against mine, his beard trailing down my neck, making me shiver all over.

"What do you say, *mia bambina*?"

"That's a low blow..." I opened my eyes, gripping his shoulders, trying to find all my self-control. "Dinner, you said we were going to have dinner... dinner...."

I kept repeating when clearly all I wanted was to be his dinner.

"We could skip straight to dessert." His eyes never left mine.

"No, I promised myself I wouldn't do this anymore." With all my self-control, I pushed him back to his place. "This... this is better..." I cleared my throat, pulling in a ragged breath.

"You still haven't given me my answer. You have until the end of our dinner to respond." Matteo started the car, pulling out of the driveway.

I knew he would want an answer, but at that moment, all I wanted was to return to my normal breathing and stop thinking about those Italian lips between my legs. *Damn it!*

CHAPTER THIRTY-ONE

Billie

"Are you satisfied?" Matteo raised his hand, brushing just below my lip as if removing the residue of the ice cream I had ordered for dessert.

"At the beginning of the pregnancy, I had a lot of nausea. Now it seems that all the nausea has turned into cravings, a desire to eat." I looked up at him, seeing him bring the tip of his finger to his lips, gently sucking on the ice cream he had taken from below my lip.

He was clearly doing that to provoke me, testing my limits, seeing how far I would go. As if hypnotized, I watched his actions.

"Our dinner is coming to an end, and I still haven't gotten my answer," Matteo said.

I grabbed my phone, opening the notes app and writing *"Rules for Coexistence."*

"Did you forget about the rules? I will only agree if you adhere to all the rules we set," I declared, showing him the notes app I had opened.

"Great, then you can start with your rules, and I'll tell you if I agree or not."

"First and foremost, no bringing any of your conquests into that house, regardless of whether I'm there or not," I said, writing it down on my phone as I spoke.

"That goes for both of us." I looked up at him again. "After all, wasn't I the one who was trying to have a date with one of the Cosa Nostra members?" His comment ended with a grumble.

"Fine, there must be a hotel nearby, or you can point me to a few," I said, trying to annoy Matteo a bit.

"Yes, I can personally take you to one and maybe even test them out, or better yet, we could have an orgy..." He clicked his tongue, stepping into the middle of my teasing.

"I don't do that kind of thing with you." I lowered my eyes, trying not to look at him, trying not to see the explicit gleam in his eyes.

"You don't because you're jealous of seeing me with another woman, but I don't judge you. I'm also incredibly jealous of you." I raised my gaze, immediately feeling tormented. He looked at me so intensely that it felt like his gaze was stripping me bare.

"You're so presumptuous. What I meant is that I don't do that kind of thing in general anymore." I rolled my eyes.

"And am I supposed to pretend to believe that?"

"Do what you think is best," I grumbled, ignoring that topic. By the end of the night, I could say goodbye to my underwear from how excited I was by that man. "Second, no sex, no touching, no long-distance conversations..."

"Is this serious? What do I lose if I break this rule?" Matteo interrupted my typing on the phone.

"Well, it depends. You might lose my company." I forced a smile.

"That's nonsense. I'm not going to stay away from you. I'm dying to touch your belly and feel our daughter, and under this rule, I won't be able to do that." The exasperated way he spoke made me smile, a spontaneous smile imagining how protective that man would be as a father.

"Alright, I'll make an exception here, except for touching the belly to feel Felicity." I hadn't realized that was the first time I had revealed our daughter's name to him.

"Wait, she already has a name? And you didn't even tell me?" Matteo grumbled, sounding irritated.

"Sorry if until a few hours ago you didn't even want to know about us. Now that you do, do you have a problem with the name?" I raised an eyebrow.

"No, the name is nice. I just didn't want to find out like this. Is there anything else I need to know?" He asked, sounding concerned.

"Nothing that I can remember." I shook my head. "Are we agreed on the second rule?" I returned to the main topic.

"I'm not, but is it worth arguing with you? No, I've realized you're always right." He rolled his eyes while keeping his attention on me.

"With time, you'll learn." I gave a small smile, running my hand through my hair and tucking it behind my ear.

"Luckily, rules are made to be broken."

"We'll see about that," I grumbled, finishing writing the second rule.

"I want to talk about the third rule," he began, drawing my attention as he spoke. "We'll be completely open about our daughter; I want to be actively involved in her life. And I'll state the fourth rule as well: everything related to you will go through my ears..."

"That's not a rule, that's clearly you wanting to intrude on my life," I retorted, disagreeing with rule four.

"I want to take care of both of you..."

"No! You want to take care of our daughter."

"And what about your support network? You'll need me," he continued insisting.

"Fine, I'll add a note: I'll have you as my support network during the forty days of my postpartum recovery, being my pillar. Is that good enough?"

"Clearly, it's not. Just forty days?" Matteo's eyes widened at me.

"For a man who fears marriage, you seem to want to become a husband without marriage," I grumbled at his crazy talk.

"I have an urgent, growing need to keep both of you safe. It's like I can't control myself. I've never experienced this before, and it's madness because when Juliana left my life, it was just drinking and anger at her moving on quickly, not at the fact that she was with another man, but at her moving on. Now it's different..." His sentence trailed off as he seemed lost in his thoughts.

"If you say you're in love with me, know that I won't believe it," I declared with a mocking smile, trying to break his moment of anguish.

"It took me a long time to fall in love with Juliana. How could I fall in love with someone I don't even know well?" He looked at me, still confused.

"Well, they say there's love at first sight. I'm not to blame for being extremely charming," I continued, still teasing.

"Maybe you're my opposite, and that's why I feel strangely enchanted by your craziness," Matteo said, and I lowered my face, feeling it burn from the heat that ran through me.

I adjusted rule four, and we continued setting our rules, leaving room for new ones that might arise as we lived together.

"And now, can I have my answer?" Matteo asked, and I bit the corner of my lip.

I looked at the ten rules we created. Deep down, I knew I wanted to be with him, to be with the father of my daughter.

"Yes, I'll move in with you." This could be the start of a new life for me and my little Felicity.

CHAPTER THIRTY-TWO

Billie

"I don't know much about this place, but I know we're not going to Yulia's house." I turned my face, seeing a small smile on Matteo's lips. "With that little smile, I'm sure we're not heading to the Vacchiano house. Where are you taking me? I shouldn't be worried, should I?" I furrowed my brow, confused.

"We're going to our home..."

"Are you crazy? What do you mean, our home?" I cut him off, somewhat alarmed.

"*Baby*, my house is now your house." Great, now I had to deal with my pregnancy hormones and the father of my child making advances.

"That sounds so married. Are you sure this is what you really want?" I rubbed my legs, feeling them start to sweat.

"What I want, I don't know. I just know that I want you and my daughter under my roof." His house had a slightly longer route than the Vacchiano residence.

"I don't have clothes. What am I going to wear?" I continued making excuses.

"We'll figure it out." He shrugged.

I crossed my arms and remained silent. A part of me was desperately wanting to go to his house. That dreamy part imagined how perfect our family could be. Me, him, and our little one—until reality set in and I thought about how he wanted me there for our baby and how he could change his mind at any moment. Making it seem like I wouldn't be able to handle it.

Everything was so uncertain, walking alongside Matteo and having no certainty, as if he were an enigma.

The car slowed down, and the garage opened, where I spotted another vehicle parked. He had two cars: the one we were in was a sports model, and the other was an SUV, more like a family car.

"You know what amazes me the most?" I asked as Matteo turned off the car, everything becoming slightly dark with the dim light, and he turned his face.

"What?" he inquired. I heard the sound of his door opening and did the same.

But he hadn't turned on the garage light, and as I got out of the car, I held onto the side of it, unsure where to go. A little squeal escaped my mouth when I felt strong hands gripping my waist.

"Damn, doesn't this place have lights?" I raised my hand trying to find something, and all I found was Matteo's strong chest.

"It does, but out of habit, I forgot to turn them on," his voice was a whisper, a rasp that hit the middle of my thighs.

"Habits that need to change," I grumbled, pressing my hand against his shirt, letting out a heavy sigh and feeling trapped.

"I just wanted to help you. Don't you want my help?" His voice was close to my ear, and I closed my eyes, slightly parting my lips.

"It would have helped a lot if you had turned on the light," I murmured, gripping his shirt tighter, feeling my nail scratch his chest. "Hairy Italian, you're breaking the rules..."

"I love breaking the rules." Matteo nipped at the tip of my ear, allowing a low moan to escape my mouth. "But we're not going to do anything..."

He stopped, easily holding my hand and reminding me that I had legs, so I started walking. Approaching a door, Matteo opened it, bringing a bit of light into the space.

I entered the large living room. The ornament I had broken was no longer on the floor. Did he have staff? He must have, considering the house was enormous.

"What were you going to say? Before you suddenly lost control of your speech?" he asked, turning around and releasing my hand.

"Oh, right... if you keep breaking the rules, I'll start doing the same. I love these little games," I retorted, taking off my heels and leaving them in the corner of the room. I let out a sigh of relief when my feet touched the floor.

"Do those heels hurt you?" he asked, genuinely concerned.

"They didn't use to, but as the weeks go by and my belly gets bigger, my feet sometimes swell, like now." I lowered my face, trying to see my toes but being hindered by the size of my belly, so I had to lift up slightly to see them. "They're swollen..."

"What do you do to fix it?" he asked, interested.

"Sometimes I call a massage therapist; it helps relieve the pain." I shrugged.

"I can do the massage if you want," he said. Immediately, erotic images flashed in my mind. Obviously, that wouldn't be good, not when I was practically climbing the walls with hormones out of control.

"No, better not." I shook my head in refusal.

"Are you scared?" Matteo raised an eyebrow as if mocking me.

"It's more about being cautious. Your hands don't know their limits, and before you know it, they're touching places they shouldn't." I started walking through the house, looking around. Everything was so beautiful.

"So, theoretically, you're afraid of yourself when you're near me," he said, following me as I headed for the back door.

"I'm pregnant, I haven't had sex in over five months, my hormones are out of control, so any touch from you makes me want to explode.

But that's not me; it's a version of me overloaded with crazy hormones." I turned the key in the double doors there.

"Should I be happy about this? Or afraid of being attacked?" he remarked as I stepped outside.

My eyes swept over the place. It was beautiful, incredibly beautiful. There was the ocean at the end of the property, unlike Yulia's house with its dividing rocks. Here, there was lawn leading straight to the sand, and the pool had blue lights on. Next to it, a small area with a table on a deck.

"I don't intend to attack you. After all, I have two hands and a nice consolation prize to relieve the tension," I teased, lifting my face and feeling his scent touch my senses as the sea breeze passed over him.

"Now I'm jealous of that consolation prize," Matteo looked down.

With that backdrop, I was even more fascinated, enchanted by the mobster's appearance. Even though he always had that cruel scowl, he had a beautiful, seductive gaze.

"Don't be jealous. It doesn't do half of what this place can offer," I teased, lowering my gaze down his body.

"You complain about me but end up doing the same thing," he grumbled, taking a step toward me.

"No sex, hairy Italian." I turned, hearing his voice huffing, and entered the house, looking around. "Where will my room be?"

"Come, I'll show you." He gestured with his hand for me to follow him toward the stairs.

As we climbed the stairs, I took the opportunity to text Yulia that I wouldn't be staying at the house but assured her that nothing sexual would happen.

CHAPTER THIRTY-THREE

Matteo

Exhausted after a night of barely sleeping, knowing that Billie was right there, under my roof, and not being able to do anything left me on edge. I wanted to get out of bed at every moment just to watch her sleep. But doing that would be madness, even for me.

Part of me struggled to believe that Billie could be my downfall, while the other part shamelessly declared that she was exactly what had been missing in my life.

A woman full of life, yet in need of attention. Attention that I wanted to give her.

It was like a glass of cold water in my face, a shock to reality. I wondered what had happened to me, how she had managed to cross my barriers with so little effort.

Damn, I was about to lose my mind.

I buttoned up my shirt, left my room, and as soon as I closed the door behind me, my eyes were drawn to the sight of the barefoot woman. Slowly lifting my gaze from her legs, the shirt that was too big for her stopping mid-thigh, and there, in the center, her belly, with the nipples showing through the fabric revealing she wasn't wearing a bra. When my gaze met hers, Billie deliberately moistened her lips. Her blue eyes vibrated with the desire that was evident in every movement she made.

"Good morning, Italian. Did you sleep well?" Her voice was a bit hoarse, revealing that she had, unlike me.

"Great..." I grumbled. "I don't remember leaving a shirt of mine in your room." I forced my gaze.

"Oh, it's not yours. I went downstairs and asked one of your men for the shirt he was wearing. In exchange, I gave him a little something," I immediately growled, clenching my fists, turning ready to commit homicide.

Billie suddenly burst into loud laughter, even bringing tears to her eyes, which made me walk toward her, grabbing her shoulders and pushing her against the wall.

"Don't joke with me," I growled, gripping her shoulders a bit tighter than I should have.

"Oh, you know I love to joke," she said defiantly, not breaking eye contact. "Did you think I'd come live here and stay silent for you? Your thoughts were very, very wrong..."

"Billie Harris, what you don't understand is that you're mine. I'm capable of killing any man who dares to touch you. You're mine, damn it!" If I hadn't scared her before, I surely did when I punched the wall beside her.

"Matteo!" The way my name came out of her mouth made me freeze, look deeply into her eyes, and blink several times until I realized I was being aggressive with Billie.

I quickly released her, taking a step back, dazed.

"I... I... apologize," was all that came out of my mouth as I turned and headed for the stairs, descending quickly, my eyes clouded, fear written all over them.

I stopped outside, panting, took a deep breath, clenched my hands, and looked out at the sea in the distance, while sounds of gunshots echoed in my mind, my mother's scream. I placed my hands behind my head, clasped my fingers, and brought my elbows forward, covering my ears.

I just wanted to lose myself, to be overwhelmed by that feeling of guilt. In the first moment, and in our first time together, I had acted that way with Billie. I was a monster.

I quickly opened my eyes when I felt fingers touching the fabric of my shirt. I looked down and saw the most beautiful girl standing in front of me.

Of all the times Juliana had been with me, I had never lost my temper with her. It was always calm. She knew me and didn't test me; maybe that's what had cooled our relationship.

"I forgive you," she whispered, holding my wrists and lowering them, making me hear her more clearly.

"I'm a monster, I lost my temper," I murmured, not moving.

"I'd say you're more jealous." She moved closer to me, raising her hand to touch the side of my face, over my beard. "Would you hit me, Matteo?"

"I'd never be able to even lay a finger on you, but what if I lost my temper?" I murmured, closing my eyes and feeling her hand caressing me.

"Have you ever hit a woman?"

"Never," I answered, meeting her gaze.

"So why do you think you could hit me?" Billie's voice was calm, speaking in a soothing tone as if she wanted to calm me.

"Because of him, because of my father," I said as she took my hand.

"You're not him, and I think you've been told that before, but I'm sure you'd never do such cruelty to any woman. You're living through the torments of another person when you're clearly an honorable man." Billie guided my hand to her belly.

I lowered my gaze when I felt that small movement, like a little wave. She guided my hand, which almost covered the entire length of her belly.

"Mornings and nights before falling asleep are when she moves the most," she said, making me fascinated by it.

She was already moving; my daughter growing inside her was making movements. I raised my other hand and touched her abdomen, almost covering it completely with both hands. It was surreal; it was my daughter, my little one.

I blinked several times, lifting my eyes to Billie.

"This... this is fantastic," I murmured, unwilling to remove my hand from her belly, wanting to feel more and more of that sensation.

"The first time I felt her kicking, I thought something was wrong. I was so scared that I even went to see my obstetrician, and I only calmed down when she did the ultrasound and showed me that Felicity was just kicking like a healthy baby." Her eyes filled with tears; it was clear that Billie would be the best mother our girl could have.

"You're amazing, Billie, the most incredible woman I've ever met," I said, lifting one of my hands without removing the other from her belly to touch the corner of her face, watching her close her eyes and surrender to my caress. "I could spend every day with my hand on your belly just to feel her kicking."

"You know, hairy Italian, she's still inside me, and that would mean staying glued to me, and no, that wouldn't be nice." Billie opened her eyes in a teasing manner.

Our tense mood suddenly lightened, as it should have been since we woke up.

"I'm starving; can we go eat?" she asked, turning around, still wearing that shirt that fascinated me with her legs exposed.

"Yes, Doroteia must have prepared breakfast..."

"I knew you had staff; it's impossible for this house to always be this well-kept," she declared more to herself than to me.

We continued walking side by side, but the episode of my uncontrolled jealousy still echoed in my mind. Maybe I should seek some advice from Valentino about this.

CHAPTER THIRTY-FOUR

Billie

Yulia helped pack my bags, getting them ready for when I would return to Matteo's house at the end of the day with him.

"Friend, this is tormenting," I complained, sitting on the bed.

"I know exactly what torment you're talking about." Yulia rubbed her belly, smoothing over the twins and gave me a mischievous smile.

"That man, he's huge, everything about him attracts me, and... I'm feeling needy." I slumped my shoulders.

"It's best you stick to your consolation, or you'll end up being consoled by the mafioso," Yulia teased.

"I wish, if only he weren't such an asshole. But we know that man could explode at any moment, like this morning." I recalled the incident, which I had already shared with my friend.

"Well, in the matter of jealousy, I'm well-versed with a super-jealous husband." When I told Yulia what happened, she wasn't even startled or impressed, considering her husband acted the same way. "Even though Matteo lost control, I don't believe he would ever do anything to you. His fear only shows that he cares, that he knows he won't do anything."

"At least I learned not to toy with the mafioso's jealousy." I gave a brief smile, rising from the bed.

I GOT OUT OF THE SHOWER, and I had a room just for myself, with a walk-in closet, an en suite bathroom, and a soft, comfy bed. My bag was open on the bed; I went to it and grabbed one of my light fabric shorts and a tank top, not wearing a bra.

Voices raised on the first floor made me furrow my brow; curiosity got the better of me. I crept to the door, slowly stepping out of the room.

I stayed out of sight, on tiptoe, stopping near the stairs where I could clearly hear what they were saying.

"I want you to leave; you're not welcome in my house if you maintain that opinion!" Matteo sounded exasperated.

"You'll make the same mistake I did; we're cursed by the damn De Luca gene. You'll end up killing that woman sooner or later." I didn't recognize that voice, but everything pointed to it being his father's.

"Even so, I want to try; I'll do everything possible and impossible to keep Billie and my daughter by my side forever," Matteo's voice was firm, but what terrified me was that man's continued doubts about Matteo.

"You're ruining your life, destroying it. You have the chance to move on and not make the same mistake I did, but you prefer to keep your eyes closed. You're going to ruin your life," he repeated with chilling conviction.

"I'm not you; my life isn't yours. Don't compare me to your mistakes," Matteo now sounded like he was growling. "I politely ask you to leave my house, disappear from my life as you always have, hide in your home, and forget about me."

"Don't say you weren't warned. Don't come running to me when all the shit hits the fan; I'm not going to clean up your mess." The man seemed to be walking away.

After a few seconds, the front door of the house was opened. If that was Matteo's father, he didn't even bother to get to know me; he just reduced me to a *mess*.

Knowing that Matteo was now alone downstairs, I approached the stairs, jumping a little when I looked down and saw him impulsively punch the coffee table, shattering it into pieces of glass. Scared and concerned for him, I descended the steps.

I approached him, our eyes meeting through his disheveled hair.

"Matteo," I said, alarmed to see blood running down his hand.

"Stay away from me, Billie! Stay away," he growled irritably.

"No, I'm staying; you're not alone now. I'm here, and I want to help," I spoke calmly, stopping in front of him. He didn't say anything, his breath ragged. I took his large hand, seeing the small cut from which tiny red droplets were oozing.

He didn't refuse the help, didn't push me away.

"Is there a first aid kit here?" I asked.

"In the kitchen..." he gestured toward the kitchen. I passed my hand over his wound, pressing it without feeling disgusted by the blood, to stop it from bleeding.

We went to the kitchen, where he sat on a stool, replacing my hand with his own to stop the bleeding. I grabbed the small first aid kit, approached Matteo, who remained seated while I stood between his legs. I took out some gauze and antiseptic from the kit.

"Was it your father?" I asked finally, wanting to fill the silence with our voices.

"Yes," was all he said.

"I don't agree with anything he said." I lifted my eyes while cleaning the wound and found his fixed on me.

"Am I making a mistake, Billie? I'd never forgive myself if I did something to you," he said, his voice filled with concern.

"Are your fears related to weapons? Leave them in the car, at Valentino's house, somewhere less visible when you're here. But from the bottom of my heart," my voice was soft and calm as I finished cleaning the wound, picking up a bandage with my fingers and placing it over the injury, which no longer dripped, I looked at Matteo. "I believe you would never harm me or our daughter. On the contrary, I think you'll be a very protective and jealous father."

I finished by biting my lip, remembering the episode from earlier that day. I applied the bandage and looked back at him.

"It's done." I smiled warmly, feeling a mix of pain and pity for him. After all, he had just heard his own father accuse him of killing his daughter's mother.

"Billie." He got up from the stool. "Thank you for taking care of my hand and calming the situation. I think I would have broken the entire room otherwise."

"I may be a little crazy, but I know how to be a good friend and a great person to lean on..."

"Oh, I don't just want your friendship, and certainly not just your shoulder. It's better not to come with that friendship talk when everything I want with you goes far beyond that," he declared for the first time, opening a smile after the incident.

"Obviously, we had to end with one of us making a move on the other," I rolled my eyes playfully.

"How could it not end this way with your so inviting, pointed breasts... calling me to squeeze them?" Matteo moistened his lips, his gaze fixed on my breasts.

"My nipples have become very sensitive, and my breasts are huge and heavy with the pregnancy, so I avoid wearing a bra when I'm at home," I murmured provocatively, running my hand over my nipple just to tease him, then turned and headed for the stairs. "You'd better get used to this view, because I walk around like this a lot."

Without turning to face him, I gave a forced laugh.

"You'll pay for this, Billie Harris. I'll be walking around in just my underwear and with a hard-on!"

"I'm sure I'll love the view," I teased, climbing the stairs and feeling the spot between my legs so wet, begging for attention.

And that's exactly what I was going to do—give myself a treat.

CHAPTER THIRTY-FIVE

Matteo

H*ell!* I threw the covers aside, giving up on sleep, and my feet hit the floor. I walked out of the bedroom, stopping still, my eyes fixed on that door, her bedroom door.

I swallowed hard, unable to contain the wolf howling inside me, and walked towards it. I touched the doorknob; the door was open. Silently, I entered the room where Billie was sleeping.

She was under a thin blanket, clearly visible in the way she lay. The bedroom window was open, allowing the sea breeze to blow in, and the moonlight that slipped through the curtain illuminated the delicate face of my daughter's mother.

Daughter, I had a daughter...

Thinking about it sometimes still left me confused. What would she be like? Small traits of mine and her mother's; I imagined holding the little one, hearing her cries echoing through the house. It might even be madness, but all I wanted was to experience every stage of Felicity's life.

Billie stirred in bed, not giving me time to retreat quickly. Her eyes opened in terror.

"Damn it!" she sat up in bed, running her hand through her hair. "What a scare, what are you doing here, Matteo?"

Her voice was hoarse, revealing that I had just woken her from a deep sleep.

"Sorry, I couldn't sleep," I whispered, telling the truth. "I couldn't stay away; I needed to see both of you..."

"This is crazy, you look like a lunatic standing there." Her eyes dropped to my fingers as if checking that I had no weapons in my hands.

"I'm not armed," I retorted, responding to her look.

"If you were, I would definitely be running out of here..."

"You know if I really were, there would be no running." I gave a brief smile.

"Makes sense," Billie murmured, lying back down in bed. My eyes traced the blanket as it slipped down, revealing her exposed belly. I took a step toward her. "What do you think you're going to do?"

"There's a rule that allows me to touch our daughter," I declared, stopping beside the bed, finding a small space on the mattress to sit.

"Matteo, it's the middle of the night. Why don't you go back to your bed?" she asked with a loud sigh.

"Just let me touch her," I pleaded and waited for Billie's approval.

"The problem is that to touch her, you need to touch me." Our eyes met until she finally spoke again. "Okay, okay, you can touch her, but then you can go back to your room..."

Without her finishing her sentence, I touched her. My hand covered her belly; she had warm, smooth skin. I brought my face close to her belly, pressing my ear against it as if I could hear something.

An instant smile spread across my lips when I felt a small movement from her.

"Talk to her," Billie whispered.

"Hello, my little one," I whispered, feeling a new kick against my ear as if she recognized me and responded. "I promise to protect both of you forever..."

My voice trailed off as she responded with another subtle kick. I turned slightly and kissed Billie's belly, knowing that inside her was growing the best gift a man could receive. The very one I had always refused to have, and now I was going to get—I would have a daughter.

"Matteo?" Billie whispered my name. I lifted my eyes to meet hers. "You can go to your room now."

She whispered, and I knew that Billie was starting to give in to my touches.

"Yes." I got up from the bed but didn't take my eyes off Billie. "Thank you for letting me touch her..."

"Theoretically, it's a favor I need to do." Billie turned in bed, pulling the covers around her and facing away from me.

It was time to leave, to face the reality that seducing Billie wasn't as easy as I thought it might be.

Letting out a sigh, I headed for the door. I knew I didn't want to leave, but it was necessary. I couldn't miss the chance to have the mother of my child by my side; I needed to take it slow with Billie.

"Italiano?" I turned around like a kid when the girl he was in love with called him... in love?

"Yes?" I tried to erase that word from my mind.

"Do you want to sleep with us?" She sat up in bed, looking at me with those lazy, clear blue eyes.

"You don't need to ask twice." Inevitably, a smile lit up my lips.

I walked back to the bed, taking the opposite side. Billie lifted the covers for me to get under them. I brushed my shirt's fabric, removing it.

"Did you really need to take off your shirt?" Billie grumbled as I lay down under the covers.

"Well, you're wearing a short shirt; it's only fair," I whispered, facing her.

"It's my bed, so it's only fair." Our eyes didn't look away from each other.

"Can I hug you?" I asked, wanting her to turn towards me.

"That wasn't the intention when I called you to lie down here..."

"It's not like we haven't touched each other before," I teased, moving closer to her. I held her waist, and my fingers brushed the side of her belly.

"It's different, and you know it..."

"Your body is still the same, and the desire I have to take you in my mouth remains the same," I whispered, my voice coming out a bit rough.

Billie rolled her eyes and turned in bed, trying to ignore what I said. I easily pulled her body closer, pressing her against my chest.

"You're so small; you fit perfectly against my chest," I whispered, pushing her hair to the side and blowing in her ear. "You know, Billie, I wanted to punish you for making me jealous this morning..."

"Italiano," she grumbled, containing herself. "What would this punishment be?"

She wanted me to say it all so she could torment herself with my voice.

"Better than talking about it would be to put it into practice." I moved my hand up, my fingers touching her breast.

Damn! They were really heavy, hard... Unable to control myself, I squeezed them firmly and heard Billie's little gasp.

"Matteo! You bastard... what the hell was I thinking bringing you here to sleep with me?" Billie turned in bed, our eyes meeting. "I can't take it anymore..."

"I need to fuck you hard," I growled, my eyes trailing down her body.

"Just sex... only sex... fuck me, hairy Italian..."

CHAPTER THIRTY-SIX

Billie

I squeezed Matteo's side a bit harder, feeling his warm skin. His body pressed over mine, our mouths seeking each other with urgent need. Our teeth clashed with friction, making me gasp. I ran my hand over the back of Matteo's neck, gripping it a little tighter.

I opened my legs, wrapping them around the Italian's waist.

His tongue traced mine, touching the roof of my mouth in a soft but urgent caress. Sucking my lower lip, he traced his tongue down my chin, sliding it down the middle of my neck as if leaving hot trails wherever he went.

Without asking for permission, he grabbed the neckline of my shirt, pulling the fabric down and exposing my hard, aching breasts, begging for his attention. Matteo's thick hair tangled in my bust as his mouth took my breast forcefully, his teeth nibbling my nipple.

It hurt, oh God, it hurt so much, but in a wild way, it made me even more excited.

His hand pressed on the other breast, squeezing it while his tongue slid over my nipple. Moans escaped my mouth; I needed it so badly.

Without stopping, he moved his mouth, his tongue trailing over my entire body, past my stomach, stopping at the waistband of my shorts, which he pulled down along with my panties, leaving me completely naked.

My legs were open, demanding his touches, and Matteo lifted his gaze to mine, as if sparks were flying from his eyes due to the intensity radiating from them.

His thick hair got lost between my legs, a squeal escaped my parted lips when his tongue touched my pussy. I spread my hand through his thick hair, pressing him harder against my intimacy.

"Oh... heavens..." I whined, unable to stop as I rolled on his mouth, begging for more and more.

Matteo didn't stop; I could feel his tongue exploring every inch of my pussy, his two fingers penetrating me, claiming me as his, drawing loud moans from my mouth.

Tremors ran through my entire body. I clutched his hair tightly, my toes curling in the sheets. I tilted my head back, screaming, a liberating cry as I surrendered to that orgasm. Matteo didn't stop, he withdrew his finger and squeezed my legs to keep me from pulling away, sucking me with intensity.

"Ah... ah... ah..." It felt like I wanted to leave and he kept me there, torturing me with my own pleasure.

But Matteo only stopped when he was sure he had drained everything from me.

His body dragged over mine, our eyes meeting under the moonlit night.

"You're even more perfect after an orgasm," he whispered, lowering his face, his lips touching mine, my taste mingling with his.

He kissed me tenderly and with lust, nibbling my lower lip. I grabbed the waistband of his pants, pulling them down, feeling his gloriously hard cock pressing against my stomach.

"Italiano," I whispered between kisses as he helped me remove his pants.

I grabbed his shoulder, pushed him to the side, and without giving him a chance to say anything, I immediately straddled his lap.

"No you on the bottom," I declared with a mischievous smile.

"I think it's better this way." His large hands touched the sides of my belly. "That way I won't be afraid of hurting your belly."

Clearly, he cared about our daughter who was inside me.

"Yes," I whispered, sliding my pussy over the length of his cock, remembering how big he was, sighing loudly, ready for another round of orgasms. "This pregnancy is making me crazy for sex, damn hormones." I whined, rolling my eyes as he slowly filled me with his cock.

"At this moment, I'm thanking them," Matteo teased, sliding his hand between my legs, his big fingers touching my folds. "Delicious pussy..."

A moan erupted from the depths of my throat.

I slid slowly along his length, in and out, adjusting to his size, my eyes locked on his, my fingers gripping his chest tightly, biting my lip with intensity, while my hair fell over my shoulders.

Matteo lifted his hand and gripped the back of my neck firmly, leaving the other hand on my pussy, continuing to touch me with his fingers as loud moans escaped my mouth.

"Go, ragazza, take me as yours," he cried out, our eyes locked, sweat dripping down my body.

Matteo pushed his body forward, sitting up without me moving off him. He removed his hand from my pussy, and while sitting on his lap, I slid my hands back near his knee, spreading my legs wide, gyrating on his cock.

I tilted my head back, biting my lip, completely filled. In that position, my pussy was more exposed, and even with my belly in the way, he could still see my folds.

"Fuck, Billie... fuck, what a heavenly sight," he growled, touching my pussy with his fingers, stimulating me.

I couldn't control myself, moving in and out more quickly, gyrating on his cock. It felt as if I had been taken over by a sex goddess. I didn't stop until I reached the peak of my pleasure, whining loudly, a mix of pleasure screams.

With Matteo's powerful jets inside me and his growls making it clear that he had come too, my hands left his leg. I lifted my body, lazily gyrating on his cock just to tease him as I got off the mobster and lay down beside him.

I was exhausted. I might have become a sex-crazed lunatic, but maybe my body couldn't keep up with it all. I turned my face as I felt Matteo's hand slide down my belly, our eyes meeting.

"I'll get a clean towel for you and then you can sleep," he purred, getting up.

I watched his perfect ass, proportional to his body. He was big; that man could be considered a statue to be sculpted.

When Matteo returned, I had my eyes closed. Without saying anything, he cleaned me gently, as if handling something delicate. Out of the corner of my eye, I saw him take the towel to the bathroom, put on his pants, and even though I pretended to be asleep, I noticed him watching me. He was about to leave when he turned to exit the room.

"Italiano?" I whispered, calling him. He turned, waiting for me to speak. "Will you sleep with me? Stay here with me tonight?"

Without saying a word, Matteo approached and lay back down beside me. It was as if a whirlwind of emotions was passing through his mind. His body filled mine from behind, and I curled up in his strong arms.

My eyes closed, and given the exhaustion I felt, it was easy to fall asleep.

CHAPTER THIRTY-SEVEN

Matteo

I caressed her small body against mine, sliding my hand over her belly without touching her intimate areas, just wanting to feel our daughter.

From the soft sigh Billie gave, I knew she was waking up.

"Can I know what those hands are doing on my body?" she purred, sounding like a playful kitten. It was clear she was teasing with that factor.

"An addendum, our body." I lifted my head and kissed the back of her ear, feeling her body shiver at my kisses.

Billie didn't turn around; she just rubbed herself against my cock.

"Make me come," she murmured, pleading in a sultry tone.

"How does mia ragazza want to come?" I bit the tip of her ear, pulling down my pants to free my cock, which was hard for that little woman.

"Take me with your cock..." she gave a small grind on my cock.

I ran my hand over the front of her body, gripping her neck. Billie was completely naked; she had fallen asleep that way, which was a great torture, but strangely I slept, slept very well beside her, like I hadn't in a long time.

"I'm going to have that little ass for breakfast," I murmured with the other hand reaching her pussy, finding it completely wet. I used that honey to lubricate the orifice. "At noon, I'm going to suck that pussy and have your honey for lunch... in the afternoon, I'll indulge in your breasts until I see you come, without even needing to touch your pussy... and at dinner... ah..., at dinner, I'll eat that pussy after having multiple orgasms in various ways throughout the day, you'll be completely surrendered to me..."

Billie tilted her head against my chest, my cock touching the tip of her ass.

"Hmm... do that, do all of that..." she repeated, giving me permission to eat her ass.

I made sure her orifice was well lubricated with her own honey and began to push firmly, penetrating her tight barriers, growling between clenched teeth, as my cock seemed to be strangled.

"Fuck!" I drove in all the way, taking her completely.

"Yes... yes..." she whimpered, grinding slowly on my cock.

I didn't stop stimulating her pussy, knowing that the key to eating a woman's ass was to keep her at the edge of her pleasure, that way I'd have all of her.

I started to thrust a bit harder inside her, feeling my cock dominate completely as Billie moaned loudly, seeming delirious. I kissed behind her ear, making her body shiver, without releasing her neck.

"Say I'm the man who can make you come so good?" I murmured, not stopping the rough thrusting.

"Ah, you cocky Italian." From the side, I could see her rolling her eyes.

"Do you like being fucked like this? Like the sexy woman you are?" I kept talking, knowing she was enjoying it.

"I love it... I adore it..." Billie rolled her eyes more and more, gyrating on my cock.

"Your ass just can't be more perfect than your pussy..., but it's so tight it's like it's strangling my cock..." I declared, biting her ear again.

"Don't stop..." Billie was practically sweating from the excitement.

"I want to ravage this little ass, I'll eat it as many times as I want, and you'll give me, give me your little ass when I command." At that moment, I began to fuck her hard, aggressively.

"Yes... oh... yes..." The little one didn't stop, was surrendered, delirious in her pleasure.

Her pussy coated my finger, my cock devoured her ass without mercy. I was sure Billie would spend the day remembering who had fucked her that morning.

"Come on, Billie, come now, give me everything you've got," I ordered, penetrating her pussy with my finger, feeling it being squeezed by her walls.

Billie screamed, and I roared, thrusting brutally into her ass one last time, coming hard.

Our bodies lay exhausted on the bed, my irregular breathing echoing in the room. Slowly, I pulled out of her, lying down beside her. The little one moved, her sleepy eyes meeting mine.

Her delicate fingers touched my chest, like little sparks, keeping me alert. Everything felt strange, as if I could spend the whole day next to her, hearing her moans, seeing her smiles, or even experiencing how she was so daring.

Billie had everything I never sought in a woman, but she became everything I ever wanted. Her opposite to me excited me; I wanted that challenge, wanted to live day by day and uncover the secrets of a life together.

I turned my body, lifted my hand to push her hair back. Was it possible to fall in love with someone in such a short time? Was it possible that without much effort, Billie Harris could completely dominate me?

"Definitely, I never thought I could have sex like that." A lazy smile spread across her lips.

"Are you going to sleep?" I asked, noticing her exhausted state.

"I think I'll take a shower and possibly sleep," she gasped as she closed her eyes. "Look, honestly, I don't know what's happening to me. Shouldn't I hate you?"

"Well, you just gave me your ass, and I don't think people who hate each other do that," I teased as she opened her eyes.

"You're a big bastard, used me, found my biggest weakness at the moment. You know I'm climbing the walls because of these hormones..."

"I can use you more often if you want, I don't mind being your sex object," I declared, bringing my face closer to hers and giving her lips a lingering kiss.

"Are you going to the Vacchiano house now?" Billie rarely referred to the Vacchiano house as the headquarters; in her mind, it was just a house, though it was also our meeting place and the hideout for torturing the guilty.

"Yes, I have things to sort out with Valentino this morning," I told her truthfully. "Do you want to come along?"

"Oh, no, I need to finish some sketches I started. It seems coming to Sicily has given me new inspirations." A beautiful smile lit up her lips.

"That's good to hear," I said with a deep sigh. "If you want, I can take you to an amazing place here..."

"I want to," she responded before I could finish the sentence.

Billie sat on the bed, her blonde hair slightly disheveled, falling over her shoulders. The perfect definition of post-sex.

"Shall we take a shower together?" I asked, getting up from the bed.

"What's the chance it's just a shower?"

"Just a shower. I want to wash the body of the mother of my daughter." I walked around the bed, easily picking her up in my arms.

"Hey..." A little squeal escaped her mouth. "The bathroom is over there, where are we going?"

"To my room, the bathroom there is bigger," I said, leaving the room and walking down the hallway without putting her down.

Billie had a beautiful smile on her lips, and I was willing to do anything to have her by my side and ensure that smile never left her face.

CHAPTER THIRTY-EIGHT

Billie

I should have been sketching, but all that came to mind was that man. The pencil glided across the sketchpad, and slowly, the features of Matteo began to take shape.

He came over for lunch, and as I said that morning, he took me aggressively in his mouth, touching my pussy with his lips.

It was madness, the wildest kind, pure madness, and I was letting myself get carried away. I confessed that deep down, I was enjoying it.

I heard footsteps behind me, turned my face, and saw him approaching, removing his sunglasses and tucking them between the open buttons of his shirt, his hair was tied back.

I crossed my legs over the lounge chair where I was sitting and closed my sketchpad. I was wearing just a loose dress, my hair gently blowing with the sea breeze.

"Have you eaten?" he asked, bending down and showing me a small paper bag in his hand.

"I'm not hungry yet..." I said, watching him sit down next to me.

He placed the bag beside us, opened it, and took out what looked like a cupcake. I couldn't help but smile at that.

"I passed by my favorite café and thought of you." He subtly raised his eyes towards me.

"Of me?" I gasped as I watched Matteo place the small paper from the cupcake down.

"Yes, of you," he whispered, bringing the sweet towards my mouth. I opened up, took a bite, and felt the taste of chocolate on my lips, closing my eyes as I chewed.

"Mmm..." I sighed at the delight.

"Delicious, isn't it?" I opened my eyes to find his looking at me.

Matteo lifted his other hand, touching below my lips and wiping a bit of whipped cream that had gotten there.

"I think this café has become my favorite too," I said, watching him bring the cupcake back to my mouth.

"Eat, my sweet." The way he called me "my sweet" made me smile as I chewed on the cupcake.

"I know how to eat by myself, you know?" I said, watching him take a bite of the cupcake and making a face when I saw he had eaten it all.

"There's more in the bag." He noticed my look. "But now I want to do something else."

His mischievous smile made me realize what he was planning.

"No," I firmly denied, quickly putting one foot on the ground at a time, escaping from Matteo.

"You're going to run away from me, is that it?" he asked, a bit louder.

"You're crazy, we're outside your house, there are neighbors, we could be seen." I widened my eyes as I saw him walking towards me.

I started running, my feet touching the sand. Without losing my balance, a loud laugh escaped my mouth when I saw out of the corner of my eye the mobster behind me. Even if I weren't pregnant, escaping him would be impossible.

A squeal escaped my mouth when Matteo's strong arms wrapped around me from behind, his body covering mine. With his hands, he lifted me slightly, my legs leaving the ground as I was spun around with him in a moment of carefree fun.

"Matteo!!! I'm going to get dizzy." I closed my eyes tightly as he gradually slowed down, my bare feet touching the ground.

I turned to face him.

"No one was going to see us." The mobster's hand slid down my back, touching my butt and squeezing it firmly.

"No!" I widened my eyes at his squeeze. "You're crazy, completely crazy!" I shook my head vehemently.

"Crazy about you," he whispered, lowering his face, his lip touching mine in a slow, soft kiss.

I raised my hand, touched the back of his neck, and felt the start of his hair.

"Did you come here just to bring me the cupcake?" I gasped in the midst of the kiss.

"And would there be a better reason?" Matteo's hand tightened around my waist.

"I thought you were on duty." Our lips slowly parted.

"I am, Valentino went to the headquarters, and I said I'd make a quick stop at my house. Well, I went to the café, and here I am." His fingers rested beside my belly as if caressing it.

"I might start getting very spoiled." I blinked a few times.

"You make me want to spoil you." With his other hand, he caressed my face.

"Hairy Italian," I sighed, closing my eyes. "You've hurt me once, I don't want that to happen again..."

"And I was wrong for that. I wanted to push you away, and I acted in the worst possible way." My eyes opened.

"I still have them firmly fixed in my mind." I directed my attention to the sea beside us.

"It won't be easy to erase the image of your daughter's father acting like a jerk from your mind, but for the first time, I want to do things differently. I've never wanted to try something so different with someone like I do with you," Matteo kept insisting.

"I feel like an experiment in your life..."

"Never will be," he cut me off.

"Then why do I feel like I am?"

"I can prove it, I can make you understand that you're not." Matteo lowered his face, kissing the curve of my neck, leaving traces of his beard wherever he touched. I sighed loudly and focused my gaze on the sea beside us, unable to hold back, I soon closed my eyes.

"Hairy." I held onto his shoulder, drawing in a deep breath. Matteo moved away from my body but kept his hand near my belly.

"Would it be crazy for me to say that I can't stop thinking about you, even when I'm at the headquarters?" he whispered.

"It's all because of our daughter..."

"No, Billie, it's not." Matteo looked exasperated.

"There's something I need to do in New York," I abruptly changed the subject, despite the fact that I was clearly the same, with him on my mind at all times.

"What do you need to do there?" He raised an eyebrow, skeptical.

"If I stay here, I need to have one last consultation with my obstetrician and then figure out how I'll have my daughter here. I had planned everything about my delivery with my doctor," I explained.

"Fine, we'll go to New York, and I'll pay for that doctor to come to Sicily to deliver your baby here..."

"Matteo, it doesn't work like that." I widened my eyes.

"With me it does. I pay, and they obey. I'll pay, and that woman will come here." He shrugged casually.

"She might have other commitments," I found obstacles.

"That's what we'll see," Matteo had a surreal conviction.

"What are you trying to say?"

"That I'm going with you to New York. Didn't you think I'd let you go without me?" He rolled his eyes while holding my hand. "Wherever you go, I'll go, even if I'm away from your side, I'll be there."

I didn't say anything. Those protective words touched my heart. It had never been like that before, I had never had someone like that, who wasn't lying, because my world was being completely turned upside down.

CHAPTER THIRTY-NINE

Billie

Matteo left his house, leaving me alone with two cupcakes, saying they were to be eaten while thinking of him.

I sat at the small counter, slowly eating my afternoon snack. It almost felt like a dream, living in that bubble, as if it were our own little world.

My phone vibrated, and I saw Matteo's name. I quickly opened the message:

"Pack your bag, we're going to New York to sort out our daughter's matters as soon as possible. I want both of you ready to live with me."

It was strange how quickly we evolved, becoming almost like a couple. But that bubble was bound to burst, and I feared what might happen if it did.

Without replying, I went up to my room. My bag hadn't been unpacked yet, as I wasn't sure if this version of Matteo as a father would last. I just organized my things.

I hadn't considered that I might be living there when I came to Sicily. I only asked my pediatrician if I could travel. Even though Yulia was pregnant and could recommend her obstetrician, I wanted at least a nod from my current doctor, the one who had monitored Felicity's pregnancy from the start.

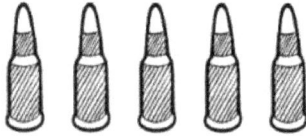

MATTEO WAS TAKING A while to arrive, so I lay down on my bed and ended up falling asleep. If there's one thing I mastered during this pregnancy, it was the ability to sleep at any time and in any place.

"*Ragazza*" the whisper in my ear made me gasp.

"Say that again" I purred, opening a sideways smile.

"We're going to travel, *my sweet.*" I felt his thumb touch my cheek. My eyes opened slowly, meeting his face close to mine, his well-trimmed beard, his hair loose and damp, revealing he had come home, taken a shower, and then came to wake me.

"It's so nice to stay here sleeping" I grumbled, wanting to close my eyes again.

"I'm not trying to ruin your sleep, but the jet is already waiting for us" he said, and holding Matteo's hand, I sat up in bed.

I lazily rubbed my eyes.

"I don't know why, but I don't feel good in New York, and I used to love that place. It's like I don't belong there anymore, ever since my mom called asking me not to come back..."

"Wait, she really did that?" Matteo seemed surprised.

"Cassandra and James always put their careers first. Why would it be different now?" A false smile appeared on my lips.

"They might feel moved by the baby. They say babies have that effect on adults" Matteo tried to soften the subject a bit.

"You really don't know my parents, *they... they...* aren't even a real couple." I cleared my throat, thinking I could never share a man with whom I was married the way they did.

"What do you mean?" He showed interest, not understanding how I meant it.

"My mother, like my father, sleeps with others out of interest. When I was a child, I didn't understand until I grew up and witnessed an embarrassing scene. They revealed to me that they had an open marriage, but an open marriage based on interest? Mom sleeps with directors or powerful men just to get information." I lowered my eyes, feeling a mix of shame in revealing that to him "I don't know why I'm still surprised by all this when I talk about it..."

"My sweet." Matteo touched my chin, making me look up at him again. Kneeling in front of me, he spoke again. "I'll never understand the whole open relationship thing, especially since I'm too jealous to share what's mine. But you shouldn't be ashamed of it. Everything you said is about them, not you. The people who brought you into this world can't always be called parents."

"I love them, or maybe I always thought I did, but it's like I've been begging for attention, for a little affection, a family night, movies, popcorn, and a lot of mess... I never had any of that with them. My nights were alone at the boarding school. Most of the girls who approached me did so because they knew my parents and thought, just like them, I wanted to be a Hollywood star." I forced a smile. "Everything I have is a repulsion for that world, repulsion for anything related to it. That's why I decided to study and graduate in something I loved."

At that moment, I genuinely smiled, knowing that I loved what I chose to study, loved everything about fashion, studying garments, and creating my sketches.

"And even growing up with all this, you never had fear. What amazes me the most is that you insist on giving our daughter the best. It makes me feel weak, weak for initially not believing I could, being afraid. I could have had your attitude, but I faltered..."

"We are constantly evolving. Just because our parents are monsters doesn't mean we'll be the same. We take our pains as examples so we don't make the same mistakes. We don't let these pains become a reflection to fear and not try. Life is one, that's why I love to live it intensely." I slid my hand over my belly, touching my little one, knowing that my great love was growing inside me. "I felt afraid when I discovered I was pregnant, but I never thought of giving up. And when I found out it was a girl, all I wanted to do was show her that I can be better than my parents were. I want to give Felicity everything: movie nights, a Christmas with lots of laughter, birthdays with every theme she wants, telling stories when she goes to sleep. I want to be her first and last best friend."

My eyes filled with tears. Having that baby was like a new beginning, a life with a little person of my own, and knowing that Matteo was by my side made it all the more magical.

"You're perfect... both of you are." He moved closer to my lips and gave me a long kiss. "We need to go. I don't want to stay there too long. Valentino authorized the trip, but I need to stop by a nightclub affiliated with our mafia. I'm theoretically going on business too."

"Everything with ulterior motives, *huh*?" I teased as I got up from the bed with his help.

Matteo didn't let me take any luggage, playing the protective father of our little one. After all, that was exactly what he was, *I thought.*

CHAPTER FORTY

Billie

The flight on the jet was smooth. While Matteo was on his phone exchanging messages with mafia men, I ended up feeling tired and slept most of the time in the seat.

Matteo wanted to stay in one of Cosa Nostra's apartments, but I didn't let him. After all, I had my own apartment and wanted to pick up a few things when we returned.

Through a message, I managed to get an appointment with my obstetrician for that same day.

I arrived at my apartment, which was just as I had left it, only organized since I had asked for it to be kept clean.

"So this is where you were hiding?" Matteo said playfully, walking around the room and looking at everything.

"Yes, more or less." A sideways smile spread across my lips.

He picked up a photo frame from the table next to the sofa.

"I took this photo when I found out I was pregnant. I wanted to capture the moment." I shrugged my shoulders.

"You look beautiful." He ran his hand through his hair, lifting his eyes to mine. "This is something we need to take to our home."

"Ours, really?" I raised an eyebrow.

"Yes, ours, mine, yours, and hers." His eyes fell to my belly.

"Italian, at some point in your life, even if it was a small moment, did you think you could be a father?" I asked, wanting to satisfy my curiosity.

"Even if it was small?" he asked as if to himself, then continued. "There was always a small part of me that wanted to be normal, to know what it was like to be a father, but... but... I always let fear win."

"At least I'm happy you considered the possibility." I smiled, taking off my high heels and letting my feet touch the warm floor. During this time of year, it was necessary to keep the heaters on. And since my account was automatically linked to my parents' house, I always kept the heater on automatic mode.

If I didn't have their attention, I took pleasure in making them pay for something I wasn't even using.

"May I ask a question?" Matteo said, looking around, and I nodded for him to continue. "Is this apartment yours or your parents'?"

"It's mine. I inherited it from my grandfather. He left a large part of the inheritance to me. I was only three years old when he passed away, and since I was the only granddaughter, just like my mother was an only child, he left part of the inheritance to me and part to her. When I turned twenty, my assets were unlocked, including this apartment and a large sum of money. Everything was blocked; even my parents couldn't access part of my inheritance. Grandpa knew the daughter he had and knew that if he didn't take that action regarding what was mine, she would spend it on her luxuries," I told him the whole truth.

"So let's say you're an heiress." He frowned amusingly.

"I have enough money to never need to work a day in my life and still support my daughter, and, oh, I have some of my luxuries tied to my parents' accounts, including the heating system in this apartment, some credit cards that, when I'm very angry with them, I go to a store and spend a lot just to remind them that they have a daughter."

"It sounds a bit spoiled to do that." Matteo scrunched his lip.

"I don't care at all. These are the ways I find to get revenge." I continued walking to the kitchen.

I heard Matteo's footsteps behind me, and I turned my face, noticing that he had a reflective expression.

"I want you to return all those cards to them. I don't want anything of yours tied to them anymore," the Italian said with a firm tone.

"What are you talking about?" I asked, confused.

"I don't want you using anything from them. You have me. Whatever you need, I'll provide for you."

"I don't need anything from you. I'm not a trophy wife, one of those who stays at home doing everything for the man." I took a glass and filled it with water from the filter. "Everything I do is out of spite. I could easily live without anything from them, but I do it to get revenge. Simple as that."

"It's not as simple as it seems. By doing that, it looks like you want to maintain a connection with them." Matteo touched a sore spot of mine.

"For years, that's what I wanted, to get their attention, as if I were screaming in my actions, 'Hey, I'm here, I exist...' but it never worked." I took small sips from the glass.

"That's what I want you to understand. You don't need that. I can be what you've always needed. I want to be your lifeline, the person you turn to when you need support, and I'll make sure to emphasize every day how important you are to my life..."

"Soon you, the hairy Italian? The same man who just a few days ago didn't want children, who had a girlfriend for years and never wanted to commit, how can I believe all this?" I set the glass on the kitchen counter.

Matteo walked toward me and stopped with his hand, soon holding the side of my belly.

"I didn't believe I was capable until I experienced all this. I thought I would be as flawed as my father. But... but... you're not like my mother, I'm not like him. I'm sure you'll be everything she wasn't. You won't kneel at my feet. You won't make me feel like I can tread on you, and as strange as it may seem, that's what I need, a beautiful, charming woman, a little spoiled but who knows what it's like to be with a man like me. I don't want your submission; I want a strong woman like you, the same one who knew how to handle me when I lost it and never lowered her head." With his other hand, he touched the side of my face. "Our opposites complete each other."

I held onto Matteo's shirt collar, his charm, his slightly disheveled but well-groomed hair. He always had a masculine scent that made me sigh every time I smelled it.

"So you're assuming I'm the best thing that's ever happened to you?" I said, leaning my lips closer to his, brushing against them.

"In my 29 years of life, I never thought something good could happen to me." A squeal erupted from the back of my throat when he picked me up and held me in his arms. "Where is your bedroom? I need to sleep a bit, but first, I need you to wear me out..."

"I think I can make you exhausted." I bit the corner of my lip.

Matteo wasn't squeezing me too tightly so as not to press on my belly between us.

"You're capable of many things, my *delicious ragazza*." We headed to my bedroom, and I showed him where it was.

Knowing it was there, and now wanting to experience all that with him.

CHAPTER FORTY-ONE

Matteo

I didn't let Billie go to her obstetrician's appointment alone; this would officially be my first appointment with Felicity. I couldn't miss it. We arrived at the office together, and at no point did I leave her side.

I was sitting in the waiting room with her.

"Do you think these women have lost something here?" I asked, leaning my ear closer to Billie.

"Maybe it's not every day you see a mobster at an obstetrician's appointment." She turned her face toward me and gave a mocking smile.

"From what I know, Valentino accompanies Yulia to practically all her medical appointments; it's not that surreal." I frowned.

I had never felt so uncomfortable in a place like that. With all those women staring at me, it was strange, even the ones accompanied by their husbands were watching me.

"But you have a tendency to attract attention wherever you go," she continued with her mockery.

"I'm just a man like any other." I twisted my lip and heard one of them sigh as I simply tucked Billie's hair behind her ear.

"You're just any man, with a beard, long hair, tall, all big and imposing. Do you really think you're the same as that poor balding guy who's probably envying your hair right now?" she whispered, making

177

me look at a man who had lowered his head in fear when I turned my face toward him.

"It's cruel to compare me to that." I couldn't help but smile at her.

"So take back what you said about being just any man; it's not quite like that." Billie shook her head.

"I don't like this place at all; I feel like I'm going to be devoured by an army of pregnant women." Billie held onto my hand, stroking my fingers.

"I already devoured you this morning, remember?" Her tone was pure sarcasm.

"If that's what you call being devoured, we can do it more often." I winked.

We arrived in New York early in the morning. I stayed awake the whole trip; I needed sleep but also wanted her to sleep with me. I made sure Billie was tired so she would be with me when she fell asleep.

We woke up in the afternoon, had lunch at a restaurant, and were now waiting for her appointment. I didn't plan to stay in the country for long, as Valentino took advantage of my need to come here, bringing with him a briefcase of weapons bought by the Swiss mafia, who also had a stake in a nightclub here in New York.

Being with Billie was becoming pleasurable; it was as if she brought many vivid colors into my life, brightening my days.

"Billie Harris?" Her name was called by a young woman.

My girl stood up, giving a nod for me to follow her, and we did. The woman who called her opened a door and gestured for us to enter; she must have been just a nurse or something...

I fixed my gaze on the elderly lady sitting behind the desk, who quickly smiled at Billie.

"I see you came with company today." The lady looked at me. "And very well-accompanied."

"It's not every day you see me with company, is it, Josy?" Billie seemed to be familiar with the obstetrician.

"Should I be pleased about that?" We sat in the chairs facing the obstetrician's desk.

"I think so, Matteo. This is Dr. Josy Mendes, she's my obstetrician. And no, we didn't know each other before; we formed this bond here. I think it's because she's seen me crying or calling countless times thinking something was wrong with Felicity." Billie spoke with affection in her voice. Now I understood why she wanted this woman; they seemed to understand each other very well. "Matteo is the father of my daughter."

"Now I understand why you called him the hairy Italian." The lady looked at me over her glasses as if she were evaluating me.

I frowned at Billie, who just shrugged.

"Well... yes... most of the times I've been here, I spent the whole appointment cursing you out." My girl pouted as she admitted this.

"And I don't doubt it." I shook my head, returning my gaze to the lady in front of me.

"How was the trip? Are you planning to stay in the city now?" The obstetrician asked immediately.

"The trip was so good that I plan to return." Billie's smile made me lose myself in it for a few seconds; she was happy, and I wanted to be the reason for that smile. "I'm here for that reason; I'll be living in Sicily. There are people who care about me there, my best friend, the father of my daughter. There's no reason to stay here, alone."

I wished she would have referred to me as her man, but we didn't label anything. What were we, besides Felicity's parents? I didn't want to be just that; I wanted much more. I wanted Billie to be my wife.

"I understand." The lady nodded. "Do you want my clearance? All the exams are in order?"

"We want you." I spoke, my English heavily accented with Italian. The woman frowned, not understanding what I meant by that. "I mean, we want you in Sicily to deliver our daughter."

"If it were a delivery in a nearby city, I would understand, but we're talking about a different country. I wouldn't be able to drop everything here and go to where you are," the lady said, adjusting her stance.

"My pregnancy is stable; you can come a month before..." Billie's voice trailed off as she pouted her lips.

"Even so, it would be a very high amount..."

"I will cover all your expenses, pay for all your days in our city. Give me your rate, and I'll pay it. Don't worry about that. If Billie wants you in Sicily to deliver our daughter, that's where you'll be. But under no circumstances will she stay here in New York alone," I interrupted, wanting her to know I wasn't bluffing with my request.

"Alright, I'll set my price, see if I can find someone to cover my shift here at the clinic, and get back to you via message, okay?"

"Yes," Billie replied, a bit more excited beside me, as this was what she wanted.

"Now, let's make the most of your presence here and do our routine check-up." The obstetrician stood up from her chair. "We'll listen to her heartbeat and take some notes."

Billie nodded, standing up from the chair, and I did the same, guiding her.

CHAPTER FORTY-TWO

Matteo

I crossed my legs, watching the redhead analyze the weapons laid out on the table.

"Everything according to what you want?" I asked, raising an eyebrow.

"Can I see, Dad?" The boy spinning in the chair asked.

"Come see, Aaron," Owen, the deputy head of the Swiss mafia in Ergänzung, who had a partnership with the Cosa Nostra, called him.

Verena, Valentino's mother, was Owen's father's sister, making them cousins.

The father encouraged his son to see the weapons, which was not quite what a boy his age should be exposed to.

"Wow, can I test it?" The golden-haired boy's eyes sparkled.

"Definitely not, your mother would skin me alive." The redhead shook his head at his son.

"How old is he?" I asked curiously.

"Four years old," the boy answered proudly.

"Isn't he too young to be in an environment like this?" I asked again.

"He is, actually. By the way, his mother doesn't know. This is our little secret, right, Aaron?" The father looked at his son with pride.

"Yes." Aaron winked at his father.

"My father used to bring me here secretly, and now it's my turn. They say we only learn through practice; one day all of this might be his." Owen seemed to admire his progeny, the same kind of look I saw in Enrico when he looked at his young son Tommie, a look I never got from my own father.

"Daddy, I don't want this. Leave it for Chase. I want to fly like a little bird, just like Mom says. Let me fly," the boy spoke like a little man of about thirty, raising his hand as if he truly understood his future steps.

"Oh God! This conversation scares me. Imagine if my only son doesn't follow in my footsteps?" He ran his hand through his hair, worried.

"As long as you're proud of him, nothing else will matter." I shrugged. "My father never cared to show me the good side of a paternal relationship."

"You know, I never wanted to have a child. My mind was too closed off; all I wanted in my life was women, as many as possible."

"But now you have a son. What made you change?"

"Polina made me change, actually. Either I changed or lost the best thing life had given me. She's as crazy as I am, supports me in everything, is by my side. It's as if she was made just for me. And brother, she's the type of woman who would take on the world for her family. Just don't step on her toes; well, I did at first, we fought a lot, still fight sometimes, but now the fights are better, they come with an extra." The way he spoke made me understand what he meant and couldn't mention in front of his son.

The way Owen spoke was as if he saw himself in my place, not wanting to have children, living alone. But now, with her, with Billie, damn it! I want to try. Not just try, I'm sure I want her in my life.

Owen finished analyzing all the weapons, with the little one constantly by his side, watching how his father worked.

"Everything is in order, then," I affirmed, standing up from the chair as I saw the deputy head nod.

"Yes, everything as requested. But why did my cousin's consigliere bring this specifically? I don't think we need to worry about any suspicion from Valentino Vacchiano regarding us." He frowned, considering that this was a task for a caporegime.

"Absolutely not. This alliance will never be at risk. You know how the Cosa Nostra is loyal to Ergänzung. I just came because I had some matters to resolve here," I spoke the truth.

"Is there something I should be worried about?" Owen crossed his arms, thinking it was related to the mafia.

"No, it's personal. I came to bring my wife to consult with her obstetrician and sort out a few things so she could have our daughter in Sicily." I was clear, making it explicit that there was nothing wrong.

"Alright, I feel more relieved about that. Are you heading back to Sicily?" He inquired.

"Yes, tomorrow morning." Moving closer, Owen extended his hand. We shook hands and parted with a brief hug.

One of the Swiss mafia men accompanied me to the exit. There were some women around, but I didn't pay much attention since the only one I wanted wasn't there. It seemed crazy because if it were some time ago, I would have been completely taken by any of those women.

There was a car waiting for me outside. I knew they were Owen's men; he had left some of his soldiers at my complete disposal.

My cell phone vibrated inside my suit jacket. It was so cold that I even wore a suit jacket, one of the pieces I rarely used in my city.

Billie's name flashed on my display. Without thinking twice, I answered:

"Billie?" I called her name.

"Matteo..." A sniffle came through the line, and my blood ran cold; immediately, my body tensed up. "Come here, come here, please..."

The way she asked made it sound like someone had hurt her.

"Yes, I'm on my way. What happened?" I needed to know; my world was crumbling through my fingers just from hearing her subdued voice, damn it!

"And... they're here," she said, though it wasn't necessary to finish the sentence as I already had an idea of who she was talking about.

"Where are they?"

"In the room at my house. They cursed at me... there was a news report, a news report with our photo..."

"Wherever they are, don't talk to them. Don't worry, you're not alone. I'm with you, I'll be there soon, okay? Understand, Billie, you're not alone, I'll be there soon," I said urgently, wanting her to understand that no matter what happened, I would be there with her.

"Y-yes..." Her sniffle cut me off, it destroyed me. It was as if a hand had reached through my chest and squeezed my heart tightly, leaving me breathless.

"I'm on my way, amore mio." As I said that, I saw the car slowing down.

Damn! Faster than I expected.

CHAPTER FORTY-THREE

Billie

I leaned against the door, my head resting on the wood. Tears streamed down my face; they hadn't even considered how their actions might affect me, my daughter, who, above all else, was their granddaughter.

How? How did they get that photo of me and Matteo at the clinic? It must have been when they called me, someone must have recognized the surname and snapped the photo, selling it to some tabloid journalist.

It was a clear photo, showing me and Matteo leaving the doctor's office, in a happy moment after hearing our baby's heartbeat for the first time. We were discussing it.

The door crashing open from outside made it clear he had arrived. I realized my mother was losing her patience with me, calling me ungrateful, irresponsible, spoiled, denouncing the day she brought me into the world just to cause her shame. I ran to my room, my heart breaking, thinking only about how my anguish might affect the little one.

I opened the door, sure it was him. My eyes searched for Matteo, and his hurried steps stopped in the middle of the room as I moved towards him. Matteo's hands quickly held my face on either side, wanting to make sure I was okay.

I always considered myself a strong woman, but when it came to my parents, I seemed to become weak. They were my Achilles' heel.

"Are you okay?" His voice came out in a barely audible whisper. A nod from me was enough for Matteo to turn towards my parents.

Dad and Mom were in the living room of my house. They really didn't expect Matteo to be what I said he was; they thought I was lying when I said the man in the photo was the father of my daughter and that he wanted me by his side.

"May every damn tear she sheds not make me punch your face, you bastard!" Matteo snarled at my father.

"Who do you think you are to talk to me like that?" James always considered himself untouchable, the best at everything.

"I could be your worst nightmare." Matteo brushed his back and, with wide eyes, I saw him unholster his gun.

Mom put her hand to her mouth, stifling a scream.

"What did you do, Billie?" My mother began to cry easily.

Matteo turned his face towards me, and without them noticing, he winked at me, then I realized he wasn't going to do anything.

"She didn't do anything." He turned back to them, like a protector for the ones who were my greatest tormentors, just as I had protected him when he was tormented, now he did the same for me. "What are you doing here?"

"This is our daughter's house, and that's what brought us here." My mother, feeling invincible, turned her phone towards Matteo.

With a few steps towards the device, Matteo took it from my mother's hand. I didn't even know if he read it, but he put on a mocking smile, threw the phone to the ground with force, and stepped on it.

"What do you think you're doing?" My mother argued again.

"Quiet, Cassandra." Dad yanked her hand away forcefully.

"Yes, obey your coward of a husband." Matteo kept his foot on the phone. "I'm going to be very clear here, so I don't have to repeat myself."

The tears in my eyes slowly began to dry as I felt protected by Matteo, the way he came running when I called him.

My parents stood there like two robots facing the mafioso who held his gun firmly.

"I don't want either of you near Billie anymore. I don't want anything that involves your names around her. This damn news, I don't give a fuck about it. I want you to go to hell if necessary, just let Billie move on. She doesn't need you two leeches who only suck the life out of her, her joy. She doesn't need anything that involves you two, because now she has me. I will do everything possible to ensure she wants for nothing. I'll be everything she needs. I'll be not just the father of her child, but also the man who will kill anyone who thinks they can come and bother her. I'm crazy, possessive, and obsessive when it comes to this woman. If I wake up and find out she's sad because of you, ah... I might even send one of my men to where you are just to deal with you two! Are we clear?"

I widened my eyes, not expecting those words. Seeing my parents in front of me was like being reminded of a sad, lonely life, the opposite of what Matteo and the Vacchiano family represented to me.

"She's still our daughter..."

"No, Mom" this time I made myself heard, walking slowly towards them, feeling brave for the first time—"You never loved me the way a child should be loved. I always hoped you would wake up one day and change, but that never happened. You never made me a normal child; I was always just your object. Please, I want you to leave this house. If 22 years didn't make you change, nothing will. You came to my home, pointed fingers at me, saying that if you lost the contract, it was my fault. Just leave me alone, let me be a normal girl for once in my life."

I wiped a tear from under my eyes. There was no sign of pity in their eyes; clearly, it meant nothing. I had only come into this world to complicate their lives.

"I want both of you out. Out of my apartment, out of my life. And if it were up to me, my daughter would never know she has grandparents. Everything linked to you two, I will make sure to unlink.

I don't need anything. I have my inheritance that Grandpa left. Even he knew what kind of daughter he had; after all, he blocked the assets until I was old enough to know what to do with my money," I shot off, catching my breath when I finished.

"So now we know how ungrateful you are." It was always about them, never about me, always them.

"Get out now. This isn't a request, it's an order. GET OUT!!!" Matteo, at that moment, aimed the gun at them amid the shouting.

Dad and Mom, if I could still call them that, left the place almost running. Without even looking back, without any regret for leaving their only daughter behind.

It was never about me; it was always only about them, never about my feelings, only their careers.

My blurry eyes met those of the mafioso who now holstered his gun and lowered his hand as he embraced me tightly. I nestled into his chest, allowing myself to cry, to cry copiously, shedding the last tears for those two.

When the tears stopped, I swore to myself I would never let Cassandra and James control anything related to me again.

CHAPTER FORTY-FOUR

Matteo

My hand traced down her back, caressing each sigh, each sniffle, wanting to draw out all her pain and anguish. Damn, Billie didn't deserve to suffer; that woman deserved everything the world could offer.

"Bambina"—I whispered with my mouth close to her head—"I'm here..."

"Promise?" she asked with a hoarse voice without lifting her head.

"Yes, I promise with everything I have inside me. I've never promised anything to anyone, but to you, I promise. I promise never to leave you, never to let anyone hurt your feelings... *unless it's me*," I said with a playful tone.

Billie lifted her face, her blue eyes dominated by the redness of crying.

"Sorry, *sorry* for putting you through this, but when I was in that room, alone, the first person that came to mind was you." Her hand tightened on my shirt.

"Don't apologize, my little one. I should be the one thanking you for remembering me, for calling me." A small smile appeared on my lips. "How about we lie down and rest for a bit?"

"You smell bad." Billie scrunched her lip.

"Ah, it must be from the Swiss club. That place has a very... clubby smell." A forced smile appeared on my lips.

"It was a real club? I didn't know you were going to a club; I thought it was a house, like the Vacchiano headquarters." Billie released my shirt and looked at me skeptically.

"The club and their headquarters here in New York, there's no house around here. I know they have a house that is the headquarters in Switzerland, but not here." I shrugged, wanting her to understand it wasn't a big deal.

"I didn't like it, not one bit." Billie shook her head negatively, which made my smile reappear.

"If you think it's better, talk to your friend Yulia. The only man I spoke to was Owen Zornickel, Valentino's cousin. Owen is married, and I bet Yulia knows his wife. She does those investigative things women tend to do and will find out that I just went in and out." I shrugged, not mentioning that the little guy was there; if Owen mentioned it was a secret, I didn't want to be the one to spill the beans.

"Investigative things women do?" Billie's face lit up with a real smile, one that only she knew how to give. "You can bet I will, in investigative journalism, I'm great..."

She shrugged away from me, as if bragging.

I quickened my steps, hugging her from behind.

"Hairy Italian, go take a shower now. Know that you won't be lying down with me in those stinky clothes," Billie said reproachfully, making me burst into a loud laugh.

"Your jealous side turns me on. You could come take a shower with me." When it came to sex, Billie always gave in, but at that moment she just shook her head, refusing.

"No way, you omitted the fact that you went to a club. I don't shower with liars." With a pout, she sat on the bed.

"Are you serious?" I asked, stopping near the suite.

"Yes, I don't look like I'm joking. These hormones might make me more inclined to sex, but know that I'm stronger than them. You can even be naked in front of me, and I won't give in." Billie pushed the covers away. "I've already showered; I don't want another one."

She wasn't angry, just slightly upset that I hadn't mentioned that the place I was going was a club.

"Ragazza?" I called in a playful tone. From the corner of her eye, she watched me. "I'm sorry, I just didn't mention it because I didn't want to worry you. But I didn't stay long, just went in and out."

"I'm not made of glass, Matteo. When you're going to do something, please, tell me everything, not just part of it. Otherwise, I'll just lose trust in you," she said what I should have anticipated.

"Alright, I'll start doing that. It's just that, well..."

"Don't come saying it's all new because we both know you've been in a relationship before." Billie rolled her eyes.

"So, does that mean we're in a relationship?" I crossed my arms.

"We're having sex, we have a daughter. What more do you want? If I find out you're with another woman, I'll cut off your dick," her tone didn't deny that she could easily do that.

"The part about wanting it to work is new to me. Before, it was more like, whatever. If it didn't work out, it didn't matter. But now, yes, it's different. I want it to work, I want to see our little one." It was impossible not to smile at that.

Billie grabbed a pillow and, to avoid a loving smile, threw it in my direction.

"Go take your shower, hairy Italian." Her blonde hair fell over her shoulder. "And before I forget, Dr. Josy sent a message. She'll be delivering my baby in Sicily."

Her smile of happiness alone made up for everything; that woman was perfect in every way, even in her enthusiasm.

"Did she mention any costs?" I asked.

"Well, I told her she could charge a fortune, and you'd pay." The mischievous smile sparkled on her lips.

"Well, if it's for your happiness." Billie rolled her eyes.

"Look at you, who would have thought, but I didn't say that. I'll give you the costs later; it's not something exorbitant. Now, please, go take a shower." She pointed to the closed door.

"Aren't you really going to shower with me?"

"No, that's your punishment for today, and there could be much worse if you keep hiding things from me." The pout returned to her lip.

"You know, Billie?" I declared, seeing her gaze fall on me. "I like your presence, and I like myself even more when I'm with you."

She simply smiled, unable to hide her shy smile.

"I also like being by your side. I really hope this dream never ends," she said with sincerity in her voice.

"If it depends on me, it never will." I winked, opened the suite door, and entered the bathroom, but before I did, I saw Billie grabbing her phone. There was no doubt she was going to talk to Yulia about that club.

And I hoped she would, she would find out I hadn't done anything wrong and that at that moment I was entirely devoted to that *ragazza perfetta*.

CHAPTER FORTY-FIVE

Billie

"I spoke with Polina." Yulia puffed, rubbing her belly.

We had arrived in Sicily in the early morning, and since I had slept late that day, I decided to come to my friend's house. Matteo wasn't at his place, and I didn't want to be alone, so I ended up coming to talk with Yulia.

"What did she say?" I turned on my side, whispering.

"She only confirmed what he told you. Polina has friends at the club, and she knows everything that goes on inside."

"So that means the Italian was telling the truth." I instinctively smiled.

He was telling the truth, not that I had doubted him, but Matteo had emphasized that everything he told me was a lie during our brief encounter in Las Vegas, which meant that it was also true.

"It's all so confusing, friend," I whispered.

"Yes, I can imagine." We were sitting on lounge chairs by the pool.

I had told Yulia everything about my parents, how Matteo had protected me, leaving out no detail.

"I'd be confused too, if I were you. After all, at first, he was a big jerk, and now he wants to give you the world." Yulia gave me one of her comforting smiles.

"I just don't want to make any decisions right now, you know, like dating, marriage. Can we just let things flow? You know that saying, 'only time will tell'?" She nodded, and my shoulders slumped a bit.

Matteo seemed like a prince, but that same prince had acted very wrong towards me. It wasn't overnight that my thoughts could suddenly change. All I wanted was to live that moment and be by his side, along with my friend. It felt like I had finally found my place in the world.

"They're coming," Yulia whispered, and I turned to see Matteo, Valentino, and little Tommie beside him.

"Uncle knew that my dad said that your son is going to be the biggest wimp the Cosa Nostra has ever had." I heard the boy saying.

Tommie was a nickname for Tommaso. Since he had the same name as his grandfather, everyone called him Tommie to differentiate the two.

"Your dad is the wimp. He should take those jokes of his to hell," Valentino said.

"Are you going to let him do that? Aren't you going to provoke him a little?" Tommie gestured with his finger, making it clear that his father hadn't said anything; it was all just to stir up trouble.

"Have they told you that you're a little devil?" Valentino teased, running his hand through his nephew's brown hair, messing it up.

"Uncle Sam says that every day." Tommie gave a punch to the side of Valentino's belly.

"I know what you want, you want trouble. What you're going through, I've been through. " Valentino laughed, exchanging a quick look with Matteo as if they were speaking with that look.

Matteo moved, bent down, and grabbed Tommie's feet while Valentino held his hands, and they started shaking him.

"NO, NOT IN THE POOL!" The boy yelled.

But they didn't even care, tossing the boy into the water with force, making him fall in the middle of it.

He sank, and I watched in horror as the two men watched the boy emerge from the water.

"My phone, my mom is going to kill me." Tommie held up his phone, showing the water dripping from it.

At that moment, two women appeared, Verena and Pietra.

"No, I can't believe it. Tommaso Ferrari, mark my words, you're going to be without your phone, second time you've done this," Pietra scolded her son.

"But mom, this time it's Uncle Valem's fault." He pointed his finger at Valentino.

"Your little devil came to say that your husband said my son is going to be a wimp Don, words he said came from your husband's mouth." At that moment, Tommie looked at his mother with a forced smile.

"Could my only child be my biggest nightmare? Where did it come from that your father said such a thing?" Pietra had wide eyes at the boy.

Behind her appeared her husband Enrico and Tommaso; the two seemed to be the same age, which was crazy considering Pietra was a young woman. Despite the age difference, they seemed to love each other very much.

"What's going on?" Enrico asked, running his hand over his wife's waist.

"Tommaso, he's what's happening. Can you believe he told Valentino that you said his son would be a wimp Don?" Pietra looked reproachfully at her husband.

"And won't he be?" Enrico squinted at Valentino.

They were obviously teasing each other; it seemed like they had some very healthy jokes.

"That's what you get when you mix the Vacchiano and Ferrari breeds; a little devil is born," said Grandpa Tommaso.

"Wow! You men are ridiculous. Matteo and Valentino can throw my husband in the pool, and my dad too. Age must be affecting their brains," Pietra grumbled at Matteo and Valentino.

Tommie, who was in the pool, got out with his clothes dripping.

"Sorry, Uncle Valem, I only lied a little," Tommie said from a distance from Valentino. "Can we talk about my phone now?"

"No, you're going to be without it..."

"Let the boy be, daughter. It seems like you've never been a child. I'll get him another one," the grandfather seemed proud of his grandson.

"Dad, please, you spoil him too much," Pietra complained.

"My first grandchild deserves everything." Tommaso winked at his grandson.

They clearly took great pride in Tommie. This type of family relationship was new to me; they argued, but like a big family, they were always together.

"Grandpa, can we plan our little scheme?" Tommie proudly approached his grandfather.

The conversation dissipated as the four of them went into the house, my eyes still wide, looking at the two men in front of me.

"Don't be scared, friend. This scene was nothing; sometimes there are worse ones," Yulia noticed my state of mind.

"This is new to me," I declared.

My eyes met Matteo's. He just winked, running his hand through his hair.

"I don't have anything else to do here. Do you want to go home?" he asked.

"For someone who almost didn't go home, you're quite the homebody now," Valentino teased, giving Matteo a light punch on the shoulder.

"Now I have good reasons to go home." Matteo patted his shoulder.

"I imagine." Valentino looked at me with a mocking smile.

He went to his wife's side, sitting on the lounge chair. Not knowing my answer, Matteo extended his hand to me, and I accepted it.

"Just because I'm tired, I'll accept your offer." I played hard to get as I took his hand.

Matteo didn't let go of my hand, walking toward his car in that way, as if we were really a couple.

CHAPTER FORTY-SIX

Billie

A Few Months Later...

I ran my hand over the side of the bed, surprised that it was empty.

I forced my eyes open and slid my hand over my belly, letting out a loud sigh at its size.

Almost there...

I was in the final stretch. The nights had grown longer, and the relentless sleep I used to have had vanished along with all my previous energy. All that came out of my mouth were complaints.

Dragging one leg at a time, I sat on the bed, lowered my gaze, and tried in vain to see my feet. I picked up my phone and looked at the photo Yulia had sent me: the tiny twins. They were so adorable; the little girl, who had been named after her grandmother, seemed to have inherited not just her name but her appearance as well. None of Verena's children resembled her as much as the granddaughter did. Little Raffaele, in contrast to his sister who had many blonde hairs, was so hairy that his black hair fell down the sides of his forehead. He took more after Yulia's side of the family.

With difficulty, I got out of bed. I couldn't wait for my daughter to be born, to have her in my arms. Her room was ready; Felicity just needed to arrive. Everything was organized and waiting for her.

My robe no longer brushed the floor as it used to; my belly had made all my clothes no longer fit.

Holding onto the banister, I went down one step at a time.

"Matteo?" I called his name a bit louder.

"I'm here in the kitchen, *principessa*," his voice sounded somewhat choked.

I continued walking, entered the kitchen, and saw him sitting at one of the counters with a piece of paper in his hand. His tearful eyes met mine, and he wiped his tears away with his hand.

"Did something happen?" I asked, concerned.

"Yes," he murmured, turning on his stool. I approached him, and one of his hands slid around my waist as I looked at the letter that seemed to be handwritten. "My father, he killed himself this morning..."

I looked up, startled.

"How?"

"I woke up to a call from one of the Cosa Nostra men, the one who worked alongside him. My father was a *caporegime*; he didn't want to retire, so he kept working, even after what he did to my mother. He was loyal to the clan. His soldier informed me that Carlo De Luca was found dead with a rope around his neck. He always said he wanted a slow death, that he didn't deserve a quick one." Matteo directed his eyes to mine, but he showed no explicit emotion, just lost in his thoughts. "When I came downstairs, I found this letter under our front door. He left it here, as if he had already decided to kill himself. Here is his farewell..."

With a forced smile, he showed me the letter.

"Do you want to talk about it?" I asked, holding his shoulder and sliding my fingers to the back of his neck.

"This is so like him. He saw that I was moving on, making my own way, not being a coward like he was, hiding in that house and only coming out to do his work. Everything he says here is shit on top of shit. If he were a real man, he would never have killed my mother, never put her through any of that. He wants my forgiveness, saying he regrets what he did, but if my mother hadn't questioned him..." Matteo placed the letter on the counter, running his hand through his long hair. "It frustrates me, it makes me angry. It's not Donna's fault; nothing justifies my father shooting her. I'll forgive him to keep resentment out of my heart, but I never want to think of him again. All the memories I had of him died with him."

Tears were streaming down Matteo's face. I raised my hand to dry them.

"I'll never let that happen to you. I want to be your fortress, Billie, not the rock that destroys you." His eyes dropped to my belly. "I promise with everything inside me, I will protect her."

"And I believe in every word you say." I told him with a loving smile.

"I'm going to handle the entire funeral. I need to close this chapter in my life. The worst thing a boy could see is his father taking his mother's life." His thoughts drifted again. "Billie, if you don't mind, I don't want my girl at the funeral. I don't want you to be exposed to that negative energy. You don't deserve it..."

"Yes, thank you. I don't like that sort of thing." That was a relief for me; I didn't like funerals.

"How did you wake up today?" Matteo always asked how I woke up.

"A little more pregnant than yesterday." I looked at my enormous belly. "I love being pregnant, but it's time for you to come out, little one..."

Matteo stroked my belly. The way he spoke to Felicity always seemed to make her more active, as if she recognized her father's hand. I felt a sharp pain from her movements.

"It's okay, we don't want a mom in pain." I held his wrist, making a face. "Since you'll be spending the day with these things, I'll go to the Vacchiano house to spend some time with Yulia and fawn over the twins while mine decides to come into the world."

"I'll take you there..." he held my hand, walking with me upstairs.

My life with Matteo was wonderful. We shared many good moments, and although we had some arguments, they were nothing serious. It was as if we were already a couple, but without the label.

What was strange was that I never knew how to address him in conversation. After all, what was Matteo to me, other than the father of my daughter?

My obstetrician, Josy, said it was good for us to maintain our relationship, but not with the same intensity as before, which I admitted I no longer had the same energy for. Josy had arrived in Sicily a few days ago. As I was in the final stretch, she visited me daily to check on me.

My intention was to have my daughter at home, with full hospital support and a nearby maternity ward if needed.

But the doubt remained: what was Matteo to me? What would we be when our daughter was born? There was a big part of me that wanted that man, wanted him with great intensity.

I couldn't imagine my life without him.

I loved him, and it was easier than it seemed to admit that to myself.

CHAPTER FORTY-SEVEN

Matteo

I didn't want to drag out my father's funeral. There was no need for it to be extended; I didn't need to play the grieving son when, in reality, I was just fulfilling a role.

I arrived home in the late afternoon, took a long shower, wanting to wash away any remnants of that moment from my body.

That silent house was no longer the same without Billie. Having her by my side these past few months had only reinforced my certainty of what I wanted: Billie Harris forever with me.

I left my damp hair loose. I knew Billie was at the office. She had sent a message saying she and Felicity were fine. After what the obstetrician said—that our daughter could come at any moment—I had become extra cautious.

I rolled up the sleeves of my shirt as I left the house, heading to the office to pick up the little one who belonged in that home.

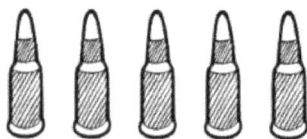

I WALKED THROUGH THE door, and the laughter of the women echoed in the room. Pietra and Cinzia must have been there as well. I first took a quick look around to see with my own eyes that Billie was okay.

As I entered, my eyes immediately met hers, my little one. Billie flashed one of those beautiful smiles that I could recognize even in a crowd.

But she wasn't alone. Juliana was there too. Given that she had been my girlfriend for a time, it was normal for her to remain friends with Pietra and Cinzia. This was the case except for Yulia, who had joined the family after I was no longer with Juliana.

"Is everything alright, dear?" Mrs. Verena asked with affection.

"Yes, it is," I nodded, heading towards Billie.

"I'm sorry about your father, Matteo," Juliana said, making me look in her direction. There was a time when I loved her, but that love was nothing compared to what I felt for Billie.

For Billie, I overcame all my barriers. I couldn't imagine that woman in another man's arms, just as I didn't care if Juliana was with someone else.

"Thank you," I responded politely. We had a relationship; all we owed each other was respect. There was no need to maintain a friendship or anything related, and I turned to Billie. "I came to pick you up to go home."

"*Oh.*" Billie gasped, frowning in confusion.

"Who you were and who you are now, De Luca." I heard Pietra's mocking tone.

"This house is so quiet without you." I winked at Billie, extending my hand to her.

But I was interrupted by Santino who entered the room.

"Well, let's put your trip home on hold for now. We need to head out," he said in a way that made it clear something was wrong.

"Did something happen?" I frowned, questioning silently. "We'll see each other later."

My eyes met Billie's; she simply nodded. Before leaving, I pressed my lips to hers in a quick kiss.

I met Santino outside the house.

"We had another attack at our cargo and unloading center. We're heading to the warehouse. We caught those damn Serbs dumping a body at our dock, and this time we know he did it on purpose. The bastards fled on a boat, holding one of our soldiers hostage. They only left him alive to show us the tattoo they made on his chest," Santino said as we sat in the back seat of the car, starting the engine.

"What's the tattoo?"

"Their dragon, with the words in Italian: *We're coming back, you worms*." Santino sighed, rubbing his forehead.

"Is there any chance they did the same with the Swiss?" I asked, knowing the Serbs had a grudge against the Swiss mafia and the Colombian cartel allied with our clan.

"None. They're not receiving any threats," Santino simply replied, confirming what I already knew.

"I believe we don't need to worry for now. We know Darko Cosic wants to take over his father's seat and will declare war on the mafias that killed his father and his men." I began to think about the situation. "He's rebuilding himself; this is just a provocation. They won't do anything, not yet, since he's still too young and lacks the experience to target a powerful clan like ours."

"Are you sure about your words?" he asked, confused.

"More than ever," I said firmly, reassuring him. "We just need to keep our men well-prepared and ensure the new soldiers are ready for such situations."

Santino nodded in agreement.

THE SOLDIER WAS SCREAMING when we arrived at our territory.

"Can't you see he's in pain? Administer some painkiller directly into his vein," I roared, getting out of the car and speaking to the men present.

Everyone was trained for this kind of situation; we had first aid kits in all our departments. As soon as my order was given, it was promptly administered to our man. I approached him, the kid's eyes wide with fear.

"There are too many of them, and they were following his orders...," the soldier, clearly terrified, continued, "Darko Cosic..."

"Damn it," Santino growled beside me.

"Let's stay calm. We'll attack when we know more about those Serbs. Acting like blind snakes running in circles is exactly what they want us to do, but we won't fall for it."

It was clearly written on our soldier's chest: "We're coming back," with their dragon tattooed there. The tattoo was fresh, revealing that it had been recently done.

"What else did you hear?" Santino asked.

"I didn't understand much. They mostly spoke in their language. We didn't leave a boat. This tattoo was done on the boat. They threw me here and left. I don't know if they'll come back. I don't know if they've already gone..."

"He doesn't know anything," I grunted, running my hand through my hair.

"We'll increase the guards at our warehouses, ask our associates to keep an eye out, and train our men with more intensity," Santino quickly took charge.

Since Valentino was with his wife, who had just given birth, and he had promised her he wouldn't go on missions, Santino was taking his place, but Valentino was kept informed of everything.

"You're right. If it's war they want, it's war they'll get," I whispered, looking at our man writhing in pain on the floor.

CHAPTER FORTY-EIGHT

Billie

I ended up coming home alone; Matteo had gone out with Santino to take care of some mafia business.

One of Matteo's soldiers brought me to our house, leaving me safely at the entrance.

The way Matteo had handled Juliana in front of everyone made it clear that there was nothing left between them—no more love, no more feelings, just mutual respect.

I was surprised when I entered the living room and felt a trickle of water running down my leg. I frowned, looked down but couldn't see anything, and touched my leg, realizing that my water had broken, or whatever it was, it wasn't urine.

Josy had said that when the moment came, I should take a deep breath and not freak out. I grabbed my phone from my bag, dialed the first number that came to mind, Matteo. He answered immediately:

"Billie, what happened?"

"Uh, yes, I think my water broke." I still felt the liquid trickling down my leg.

"What do you mean, you think? Billie, how are you? Are you still at the headquarters?" He began asking questions non-stop.

"I just got home. I'm going to call Josy now," I said, heading for the sofa, letting out a long sigh as I sat down, feeling the first contraction, which came suddenly and strongly, as if it was squeezing even the tip of my toe.

"Okay, I'm coming over right now." Matteo ended the call, but before he hung up completely, I heard him give an order to the driver, sounding almost desperate.

I called Josy, who was at a nearby hotel. She responded promptly that she was on her way. Could this be the moment my daughter would come into the world?

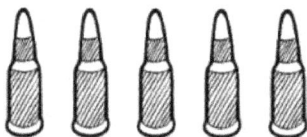

"JUST A LITTLE MORE, you're almost there," Josy said again, but at that moment, I could hear nothing more, and I wasn't processing anything happening around me.

My eyes met Matteo's; he was constantly wiping my forehead with a cloth, never letting go of my other hand. Even though I grimaced in pain, even though I cursed at him, he stayed there, strong and steady.

"I can't do this," I whined, my body numb, wishing it would all end soon.

"Yes, darling, you can. You're almost there," Josy's confident voice, which didn't belong to me, reassured me.

Nearby, three nurses were ready to take care of my daughter. My legs were spread on the bed, feeling sweat trickling down every part of my skin in that delivery room, which we had prepared with everything we would need.

"Billie, mio amore," Matteo's deep voice echoed beside me. "You're almost there; I know you can do it. You're the bravest woman I've ever known." The Italian lowered his face, his nose touching the tip of mine. "I love you madly for giving me the best gift, one I rejected for many years of my life, and you, in your finest form, surprised me..."

"Seriously, Italian?" I muttered irritably. "You're going to tell me you love me now? Now..." I moaned loudly as another wave of pain swept through my body.

Matteo just smiled, knowing that at that moment, it wasn't really me but my terrified self facing the childbirth.

As if with the snap of a finger, it all happened. Suddenly, she was no longer inside me, and a baby's cry filled the room.

"Felicity has arrived, showing us what she's made of," Josy said, wrapping my daughter in a blanket. "Do you want to cut the cord, daddy?"

The nurse showed the scissors as Josy spoke. With shining eyes, Matteo took them, though I didn't see how he cut it.

Bringing the baby toward me, the nurse lowered my daughter onto my chest, giving us our first contact.

"Hello, my little bundle of joy," I whispered, lowering my face and raising my hand, wanting to touch her.

The nurse didn't release Felicity, holding her firmly there.

The baby's lips were pursed, her cries filling the room. Bloodstains marked her reddish skin, and her eyes barely opened. *She is simply perfect, even more perfect than I had imagined.*

"She... she... is perfect, perfect." Matteo, beside me, thought the same as I did.

"And ours." I smiled, looking at that little perfection.

I SQUEEZED MY EYELIDS shut, then slowly looked up at the ceiling, feeling an emptiness inside me. Quickly, I reached for my belly. It was no longer there.

Sitting up quickly on the bed, without thinking about the consequences, I searched for my daughter, terrified. Then I found her. My chest heaved with relief.

There they were. Matteo was sitting in the armchair in our room, holding our little one against his bare chest, a tiny pink bundle. Her dry hair was turning a light brown, possibly indicating she would take after me.

"What a scare," I whispered.

"You shouldn't get up so quickly; it's only been a few hours since you brought our daughter into the world," he murmured, his eyes fixed on me.

"I just woke up scared because I didn't feel her inside me anymore. It's strange being alone." I sank back into the bed.

"You'll never be alone; I'm here with you. We're here, me and our little one." He gave me that smile that filled me with light inside, making butterflies flutter in my stomach.

"But now she's born..."

"And now we'll share her, here at home. We'll make sure this little one grows up with both her parents. She'll know what it's like to be loved, to receive affection. She'll never have to beg for anything emotionally because we'll be the foundation she needs." My eyes filled with tears as I listened to his words.

I knew I might experience mood swings, as the postpartum period revealed that other side of me.

"I know you'll be the best father for our daughter," I declared, breaking into a wide smile.

"And you'll be the best mother; I have no doubt about that." Matteo winked, still charming. "I believe she'll wake up soon to nurse. If you want, you can go to the bathroom now, but take your time."

"You're right." I nodded gently and got out of bed.

We had nurses there; two stayed to help with Felicity and me during those first few hours.

CHAPTER FORTY-NINE

Matteo

With the nurse's help, Billie was managing to nurse our daughter. The connection between the two of them fascinated me. Like a lovesick fool, I couldn't take my eyes off them.

I could say that the little one was the most beautiful thing I had ever seen in my life, but that was definitely my doting father side speaking. I now understood clearly what Valentino and Santino went through when they first saw their children. It was as if I could conquer the entire world for that little girl. *My little girl...*

The nurse who assisted Billie left the room with Felicity's changed clothes. I stood up from the armchair and approached them.

"I can see the drool dripping from the corner of your eyes, Italian," Billie teased in a low voice.

"I'd never forgive myself if I missed this moment in my life." I sat down next to them, focusing my attention on the little girl sucking at the breast.

"You're such a big softy." I looked up.

"I admit it," I joked. "You know, I'm thinking of introducing chastity rings to our daughter, making her vow to the church, so I'd be sure she stays pure until her wedding..."

"*Italian! Seriously?*" Billie's eyes widened at my overprotectiveness.

"Yes, can you imagine someone doing to her what I did with other women?" This time, it was me who widened my eyes, not wanting to picture what I had imagined. "I'd kill the bastard."

My voice unintentionally came out as a growl.

"Good thing she'll have me as her best friend." Billie rolled her eyes at my excessive act. "We're going to drive Daddy crazy, aren't we, my little one?"

The way Billie smiled enchanted me. It was her, always her, the only woman who managed to dominate my body, grip my heart so tightly that she dug her nails into it. She claimed me as her own, and that's what I wanted, no one else, just her, *only her...*

"Want a tissue, hairy Italian?" she teased my look again.

"I don't think I've ever seen such perfection in my life, you two, the two best things that ever happened to me," I said, raising my hand to touch the corner of Billie's face. "You are everything I've ever wanted, Billie, even when I was running away, even when I said I didn't want a wife, a child, you showed up, effortlessly, without making me do anything, you conquered me with your crazy ways and completed me in a way I never thought possible. My life has never been so full of new experiences as it has in these past months. I love waking up next to you, love knowing I'll spend this day by your side, and that you'll probably fascinate me even more with your sweet way of living. I love falling asleep every night with you, feeling your scent, your hair against my nose as I fall asleep smelling it. I know we haven't given labels, but I don't want to stay this way anymore. I want you to be mine, officially, so everyone knows. I want to put a ring on your finger, the symbol of our union. I love you, Billie, love you more than I've ever loved anything before. I love you madly, painfully. My chest aches at the thought of losing you. Be mine forever, *for real*, before God, before everyone.

I reached into my pants pocket, pulling out a small velvet box. With Yulia's help, I bought the engagement ring, and of course, I needed assistance to get the right size for her finger.

"Will you marry me?" I opened the box to reveal the small ring, delicate with a blue stone. "Will you be mine forever? To live until eternity if possible? To take care of both of you, to give all the love you deserve, I promise with everything inside me, I'll be the best for you both. Will you be mine forever, Billie Harris?"

Her eyes, filled with tears, fixed on the ring in my hand.

"I... I... of course I accept. I thought you'd never ask. I was so confused about everything." Felicity had finished feeding, and with my help, we removed the little one from the breast.

A drop of milk was trickling from the corner of my daughter's mouth, so enchanting and lovely, small and delicate. She lay on the nursing pillow around Billie.

I held my wife's delicate fingers. I took the ring and placed it there.

"Now you're officially mine, or at least you will be very soon." I smiled.

"You fool, I've always been yours. I just didn't want to admit it." A mischievous smile lit up her lips. "I love you, my hairy Italian. I feel safe with you like I've never felt before. It's like I've found my place in the world. My place by your side."

"You're perfect, *ragazza mia*," I whispered, bringing my lips close to hers. "The strongest woman I've ever known, the one who brought our daughter into the world, who from the start never had doubts about wanting this little one, the best mother Felicity could have. Thank you for making me a better man. A better man for both of you..."

My eyes fell on Felicity, her eyes closed, her many tiny hairs a shade of light brown. She was beautiful, the perfect blend of her mother and me, my daughter. I could finally say I had a daughter, a family. I wanted those two; I wanted them by my side. There were no doubts, only an absolute certainty.

I had become what I feared the most, and I was proud of it. There was no more resentment, no more fear. Along with my father at that funeral, I buried all my torment. I buried my demons with him.

I wanted to shout to the world, I was a family man, Felicity's father, the future husband of the most enchanting woman who had ever crossed my path, Billie Harris, my downfall, the woman who had conquered me.

"I love you, my hairy Italian," she whispered, and with that gentle tone, I knew I had made the right decision in my life.

EPILOGUE ONE

Billie

A Few Months Later...

I was nervous, my entire body was vibrating; it was the big day.
My big day.

I clasped one hand with the other, always imagining that one day I would get married, just never expecting that moment to be like this, alone. But I didn't feel alone; I never felt like I had before. Now it was as if I lived in a bubble of love. Where everyone wanted me, desired my presence.

I was no longer a burden, but Billie, Billie the friend, the mother, and now the wife. I would become Matteo de Luca's wife, the man I first met at Yulia's wedding but never paid much attention to. The same man that I reencountered in Las Vegas, whose charm and cocky demeanor captivated me, in fact, gave me an uncontrollable desire to be by his side that night. Or maybe it was just the booze that led us to this direction.

Two lost and lonely souls who reunited in a clash of emotions.

My parents had never shown up again; they simply preferred to pretend I no longer existed in their lives. They continued with their glamorous routines, appearing at many events, and when asked about their daughter, they would just say she was living in another country.

The truth is, I didn't want anything that tied me to them. I didn't want my wedding to be an excuse for a photographer to snap a picture of me and showcase it on some site, as if the Harris's daughter had gotten married and not invited them. That's why I asked for a small, intimate ceremony, just for those closest to us.

A small party wouldn't attract attention. I only wanted the people who were truly important in my life. All the Vacchianos, my husband, my little one, and that's it. I didn't need anyone else.

That was my circle; they were my new family, the people who completed me and made me happy.

"Did you really think I was going to let you go in alone?" I turned my face to see my friend approaching.

Yulia was wearing a beautiful dress in a shade of baby pink, matching her skin tone.

"I thought you were inside." I frowned in confusion.

"I was, but I came out here." Yulia stopped next to me, interlocking her hand with mine. "I'm going to take my friend to the altar. I've always said we were sisters, and you'll never be alone. I'm here for you..."

My eyes filled with tears.

"I can't cry," I mumbled, waving the other hand in front of my eyes, trying to calm down.

"You're not supposed to cry." She smiled at me.

"Who would have thought, us, two college girls, just wanting to enjoy our college years, and now we're here." We exchanged a loving glance, reminiscing about our past.

"Two mothers, one wife, and one future wife," Yulia completed.

"You were one of the best things that ever happened to me," I declared, knowing that if I could count on anyone forever, it would be her. Yulia, my sister by heart and soul.

"I love you..."

"I love you..." I declared, turning my face as the chapel doors opened, the soft wedding march starting to play slowly.

My eyes fixed on the altar, where he was, my man, my hairy Italian.

"Are you ready?" Yulia whispered.

"As ready as I've ever been..." I nodded, knowing it would be impossible not to cry.

This was a new beginning, a new phase that had already started when Felicity was born, now it would be our continuation.

My eyes went to the side where I saw my little one in the stroller, next to the Vacchiano twins, Yulia and Valentino's children. It was amazing to know that my daughter would grow up surrounded by friends, a huge family. After all, we had even moved to the condominium so I could be closer to my friend, and it was better for Matteo to work and come home whenever he wanted to sneak a peek at us.

Together with Yulia, we were working on sketches for a new collection for a well-known brand in Sicily. We wouldn't be idle; we needed to at least put into practice our many college goals.

Slowly, we approached the altar. Matteo extended his hand, and Yulia placed mine into his.

My friend stepped aside, standing next to her children who were in the stroller with Felicity. Along with her husband Valentino.

My eyes met Matteo's, and there I knew, I was sure that it was by his side that I wanted to spend the rest of my life. He who could be a ruthless mobster with his enemies, a man devoted to his clan.

Even knowing that he lived an illegal life, my heart didn't care. It always beat faster when it came to Matteo de Luca.

He saved me, took me away from that family, showed me I could be better, and he was the best.

"Are you ready to become Mrs. De Luca?" he asked, his hair styled back, his imposing gaze fixed on me.

"I can't wait to change my last name and be Mrs. De Luca... a designer, Billie De Luca," I whispered knowing that I wanted this. Breaking away from the Harris's was easier than I expected, and now it would be forever.

"I love you, Billie..." He winked as we turned to the priest present.

This was my life, my fairy tale, which at first had gone all wrong, my prince who, even though often a *bad boy*, was mine. And I loved him, unconditionally, like I had never loved anything before.

Let this be my new beginning, my starting point, with everything I've always dreamed of—a daughter, a husband, a family...

EPILOGUE TWO

Matteo

Five Years Later...

I walked into the pink room and made my way calmly to my daughter's bed. Her blonde hair spread out on the pillow. Over time, her hair had been getting more and more like her mother's.

I lowered myself onto the bed, stroking her hair.

"*Bambina mia*," I whispered.

Felicity squeezed her eyelids, slowly opening her eyes and meeting mine.

"Daddy?" she asked in a sleepy voice.

"Today is Mommy's birthday." I smiled as I watched her quickly sit up in bed.

"*Yay*!" She ran her hand over her face, clumsily brushing her hair away. "Let's make her breakfast..."

Felicity swung one foot over the edge of the bed, her pink pajamas matching her favorite color. She headed for the door.

"We need to be quiet, Daddy." Felicity put her hand to her mouth, signaling that we needed to stay silent.

I nodded, smiling. I followed my little one as we went downstairs. It was like we had created our own family traditions; every birthday of a member of our household, we would make breakfast in bed, giving my wife everything she never had, just as I hadn't. Showering Felicity with love, making sure she knew she deserved the world and never to settle for anything less.

I placed the tray on the counter. Felicity excitedly moved around the kitchen, gathering everything Billie liked.

The task of preparing the breakfast was mine. I took the small cake I had secretly bought from the fridge. Even though she knew we were doing this, she eagerly anticipated it. Ever since Felicity turned one, we had started this tradition, and it quickly became indispensable.

"Ready?" I asked, seeing Felicity shake her little head.

"Yes, let's go, Daddy." She went ahead.

I carried the tray and climbed the stairs slowly. Felicity stopped in front of the door and waited for me to catch up. With my nod of approval, she opened it.

"MOMMY!" she squealed. "HAPPY BIRTHDAY..."

She ran to her mother and threw herself onto the bed, while my wife turned with a big smile and received our daughter's hug. The two of them burst into a joyful laughter.

I stopped by the bed, my eyes meeting Billie's. Felicity sat cross-legged next to her mother, and I placed the tray on my wife's lap.

I lowered my face and held her chin.

"Happy birthday, my queen." In a lingering kiss, I joined our lips. "I love you, today, tomorrow, and always."

"I love you, my *hairy Italian*," she whispered.

"Let's eat," Felicity grumbled.

"Absolutely." Billie turned her gaze to the tray.

The breakfast was for the birthday girl, but we all ended up eating.

I sat on the edge of the bed, holding Billie's leg.

Felicity immediately attacked the sweets.

It was like watching a movie in my mind, my daughter at five years old, my wife whom I loved more than anything in this life. Billie was everything good that came into my existence. She brought her joy and brightened my days.

There was never a moment of regret; I knew it was her. *It always was.*

Felicity was the perfect key that completed us, making everything even more perfect.

There was no denying it; I never imagined living all this, and now I was experiencing my family.

I loved it, loved waking up every morning with the two women who illuminated my existence.

If I could turn back time, I would return to the exact moment we met and live it all again, with her, my wife, the only woman who had touched my heart with such intensity, claiming me to be hers. And I became hers, the happiest man of all.

THE END.

Did you love *Fate's Gamble*? Then you should read *Dangerous Affections* by Amara Holt!

Dangerous Affections

When you're the **consigliere** of the Italian mafia, love is the last thing on your mind.

Luigi, the **ruthless enforcer** of the Cosa Nostra, is feared for his **cold precision** and deadly methods. Trained in medicine to prolong his enemies' suffering, Luigi hides a **dark and traumatic past** beneath his controlled exterior. He thrives on order and lives by the rules—until Bella crashes into his world.

Bella is the opposite of Luigi in every way. She's **clumsy**, compassionate, and working three jobs just to survive. Behind her warm smile, however, she hides a **secret** that could shatter her life. When fate forces these two unlikely souls into a **fake relationship**, their worlds collide in an explosive mix of **danger**, passion, and **forbidden desire**.

As tension rises and sparks fly, Luigi and Bella must navigate a **perilous game of deception** where trust is fragile, and their hearts are on the line. Can love truly blossom in the shadow of vengeance, or will their **dangerous affections** lead to destruction?

Dangerous Affections is a gripping **enemies-to-lovers** mafia romance filled with **suspense**, steamy chemistry, and unforgettable characters. Perfect for readers who crave **high-stakes drama**, intense emotions, and a love story that defies the odds.

About the Author

Amara Holt is a storyteller whose novels immerse readers in a whirlwind of suspense, action, romance and adventure. With a keen eye for detail and a talent for crafting intricate plots, Amara captivates her audience with every twist and turn. Her compelling characters and atmospheric settings transport readers to thrilling worlds where danger lurks around every corner.

Milton Keynes UK
Ingram Content Group UK Ltd.
UKHW041950291124
451915UK00001B/92